The Greenleaf Fires

JOHN A. GOULD

The Greenleaf Fires

CHARLES SCRIBNER'S SONS
NEW YORK

Library of Congress Cataloging in Publication Data

Gould, John A 1944–
The Greenleaf fires.
I. Title.
PZ4.G6966Gr [PS3557.0865] 813'.5'4 77-17824
ISBN 0-684-15478-1

1 3 5 7 9 11 13 15 17 19 o|c 20 18 16 14 12 10 8 6 4 2

PRINTED IN THE UNITED STATES OF AMERICA

For my father

"Where there is a reconciliation,
there must have been first a sundering."

—JAMES JOYCE

The Greenleaf Fires

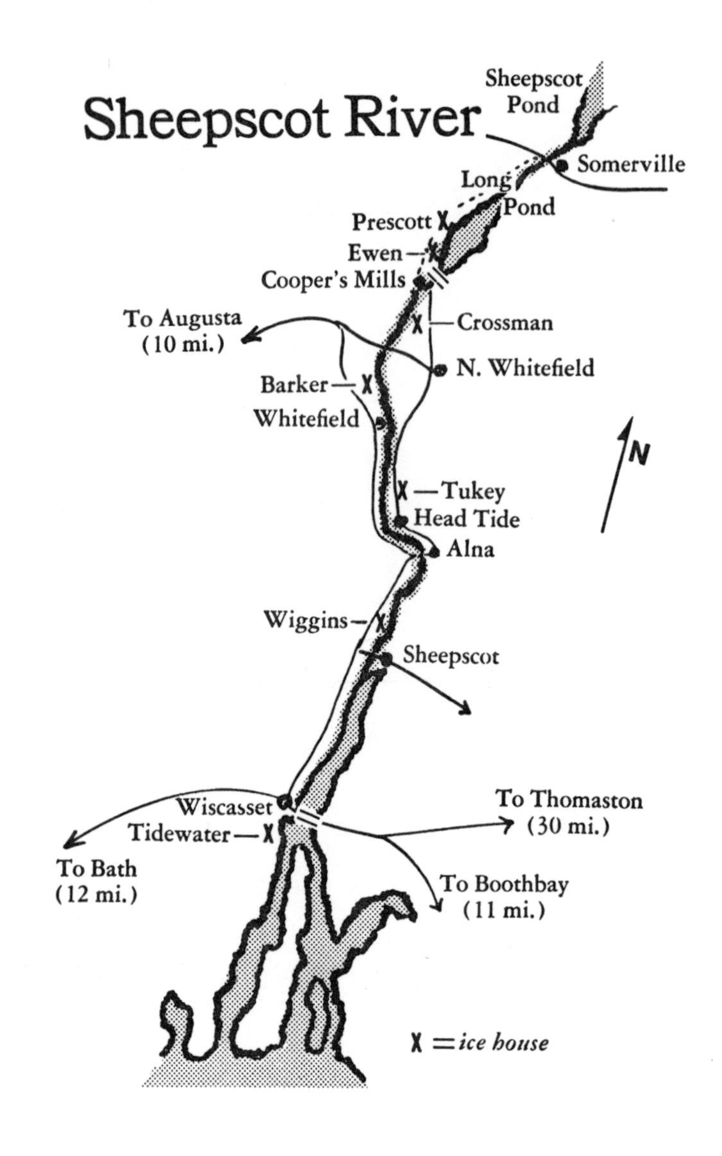
Sheepscot River
Sheepscot Pond
Somerville
Long Pond
Prescott
Ewen
Cooper's Mills
To Augusta (10 mi.)
Crossman
N. Whitefield
Barker
Whitefield
N
Tukey
Head Tide
Alna
Wiggins
Sheepscot
Wiscasset
Tidewater
To Thomaston (30 mi.)
To Bath (12 mi.)
To Boothbay (11 mi.)
X = ice house

I River

To begin, a river: the Sheepscot, originating from the southern end of Sheepscot Pond, Waldo County, Maine; at first a trickle running south through Lincoln County past Somerville into Long Pond and out, past Cooper's Mills (dam-widened now, and navigable by canoe), past Whitefield, Alna, Head Tide, Sheepscot (here broadening into a bay), Wiscasset, Boothbay, and Five Islands; reaching after some fifty-five miles the Atlantic by Reid State Park in time to demarcate Miscongus Bay on the east and Casco Bay on the west. This is map-fact, true and verifiable for anyone with either atlas or feet.

Consider now this, the river's history: called *Aponeg* by the Wawenocks, whose chief, Mentawmet, controlled the entire river in 1606; called *Sheepscutt* by the Englishmen who began buying land in 1639 from the son of Mentawmet, known as Robinhood, and who completed the purchase in 1667; called this because of the shepherd's huts which sprang up on its banks, symbolizing the purchasers' primary occupation. The first of them had the unobtrusive name of John Brown, but he and those who followed him were hardy pioneers (described by a Boston official as "the worst of men") surviving many freezing winters and two Indian massacres, one in 1676 and the second six years later. They developed industries on both land and water, selling wool, lumber, dairy produce, dockage, fish, and ice—105,100 tons in 1882—turning even God's own thirty-below winters to their advantage. By 1955, more than seven thousand people had divided, broken up, squatted over, and scratched their names upon the valley of Mentawmet's Aponeg. This is post-fact, relayed as truth through various chain letters, the originators of which perhaps met the individuals named and perhaps saw the events described.

Finally the lore of the river: *Märchen* seeming to emanate from the waters themselves—Indian legends, superstitions, even the stumper about Jean Poulin, a Frenchman from Edgecomb, who while smelting on the river with two friends, drank half a bottle of rye (this during Prohibition) and fell through the race-hole of the smelthouse only to pop up through the race-hole of another smelthouse thirty yards downstream, with a smelt in each of his coat pockets. In their way these are art-facts, and their truths are verifiable in the accuracy with which they reflect images of the human spirit. As such, they may constitute a small element of the most brilliant of all the varied and splendid orders of truth.

1

In August of 1946 seven ice houses stood along the river between Somerville and Wiscasset, including the huge old Tidewater Ice Company six-roomer on Birch Cove. On the morning of September 1, Alcott Greenleaf burned five of them to the ground.

The night before, he had stormed out of his father's house and jumped into a Model A pickup, which he then pounded upriver toward Cooper's Mills. (He and his father had recently built this truck out of the organs of at least four vehicles besides the Model A itself. "Use it until I can sell it," the old man had said; but by that time they were quarreling so regularly that Greenleaf had not until now had the chance to drive it.) It snarled and bucked along the bumpy road, and he held fast to the wheel with his one hand in furious desperation.

He roared through North Whitefield, crossed to the west side of the river at Cooper's Mills, and turned right just after Ewen's General Store. The headlight beams picked out shadows of craters in the dirt road ahead, floodlights on an unrolling ribbon of battlefield, until—*crack!*—he was thrown against the door and the steering wheel twisted from his grasp. The truck dived over the left-hand ditch and broke through a copse of young birches before coming to rest gently against the trunk of a large maple. There was the soft hiss of escaping steam.

Opening the door so violently against the maple that the leaves shook, he leaped out frothing. "Bastid!" he swore, and kicked the rear wheel. One of the headlights had survived, but he did not bother to look for the broken axle or inspect the truck at all. Reaching into a toolbox bolted to the front of the truck body, he pulled out a two-gallon gasoline can and stumbled back to the road.

There was no moon, but the night sky was clear and bright with stars. With the truck at his back, its single headlight still burning in the dark woods, he began walking quickly in the direction he had been traveling. The air was still and freezing cold. From his mouth spurted sharp squeaks of anger like steam from a boiling kettle. After a half-mile or so he turned down a road leading to the right and shortly arrived at a clearing on the edge of Long Pond. Several boats lay by the shore, among them a canvas canoe whose lacquered bottom glistened in the starlight.

Greenleaf flipped the canoe over. There were no paddles,

but he rummaged in the other boats until he finally found a pair of oars, each with its oarlock riveted to it. He carried one oar back to the perimeter of the woods, jammed it between two trees, and threw his weight against it. It bent but did not break. Tying his handkerchief around the shaft at the oarlock, he carefully poured over it gasoline from the can. From his pocket he brought his cigarette lighter, a silver-cased Zippo, and the handkerchief burst into a ring of bright fire. It burned for about three minutes. After the flames had died, he bent the oar again and it snapped at the burn. Taking up the shortened oar and the gasoline can, he strode back to the canoe, launched it, and paddled away.

Although lack of his left hand made a certain amount of awkwardness inevitable, he was able to use the oar well enough to paddle, with the throat of the blade held with his hand and the burned and broken butt end pressed into his left forearm. In less than twenty minutes he had beached the canoe a mile and a half farther up Long Pond and was staring intently into the black woods. It was then shortly after one o'clock. He looked at the luminescent wrist watch he had gotten while in the Army; "Rabbit-rabbit," he muttered, recognizing the month change, obedient to his father's superstition. Then he stepped out of the canoe.

He knew there was an ice house here. It had been built almost fifty years earlier around the turn of the century by a farmer named Gus Prescott, who was distinguished primarily by being known as the ugliest man in Lincoln County. Greenleaf's father, Eustis, had once cut ice for him. "That old baster," he had once told his son in a voice indignant with admiration, "looked like the north end of a southbound moose. Didn't smell much prettier, either. Worked me like a nigger. Old baster." Gus Prescott had been dead twenty years, the farm maintained after a fashion by his son (the old man had married at last, a union which proved to many that the gods are even in this age still active in heaven and on earth, for he had somehow uncovered less than twelve miles away a woman uglier than himself, who not only would indubitably remain faithful to him, but also—as it turned out—would bear him a son, Gus Junior, a perfect monument to their combined ugliness). Greenleaf did not know the son, but Eustis used to say that the farm had gone downhill since the old man's death.

He stumbled over the roots of great pines that loomed over him. The ice house had been built within this grove to protect it further from the fire of the summer sun, close to the pond shore, with an access road leading away from the rear. His hand went digging into his pocket for the cigarette lighter as he stomped toward the invisible building. He extended his left arm in front of him in the dark, forgetting in his distress and anger that there was nothing at the end of it (under the trees the night was so black that he could not see his absence of hand in front of his face), until his nonexistent fingers and palm slid silently through the pine wall of the ice house, and his stump suddenly banged against it.

"Bastid." Striking the lighter, he found that the door hinges had long ago rusted and fallen away, that the door itself—six inches thick and insulated like the door of a giant walk-in icebox—lay on its side propped against the opening. He leaned over this obstacle and peered inside. By the flickering light he saw the building was empty, the floor a mess of dried pine needles, leaves, and sawdust.

Reaching inside down to the floor with the flaming lighter still in his hand, he pushed some of the refuse into a small pile and touched it off. Pine needles flashed into fire, curled into red wires; light and a crackling noise filled the small room. Greenleaf pulled his arm back, his eyes gleaming in the sudden light. *Snap!* and the whole floor was blazing, quick little serpents of fire licking at the old dry walls.

With an expressionless face he turned and went back to the canoe, the illumination behind him throwing dancing shadows into his path. He put one foot into the middle of the boat and looked back just as a *whoosh!* came from the fire (the inner walls giving way released the ancient sawdust insulation, which cascaded into the room like gunpowder). Again he turned away to the canoe, pushed off, and began paddling down the pond, all the while—although he made no sound at all—weeping freely.

Gus Prescott had used his ice house to provide the cooling for milk and other dairy products from his farm. It was not large—inside measurements eight by eight by ten—and could have held no more than ten tons of ice had it been completely filled. In practice it had rarely held four, even in its prime. The only other one on the pond belonged to Frank Ewen, the proprietor of Ewen's General Store in Cooper's Mills. With interior dimensions of twenty by twenty by twelve, this one was a good deal bigger, but necessarily so: Ewen not only had used block ice to preserve the produce he kept in the store, but also had for years sold it commercially. He and his two sons built the house in 1920 about two hundred yards in back of the store and packed it with almost twenty-five tons of ice that they and a hired man cut during subzero winter days while his wife kept the store open and warm. Even last year he had put in over seven tons (although not personally; at sixty-three, Ewen's ice-harvesting days were done) and had less than three hundred pounds left when Greenleaf beached his canoe early that morning.

Compared with the air, the pond water was warm when he stepped into it to pull the bow up on the shore. By this time he was sober, no longer crying; and he felt that his despair had condensed into a pure and fine hatred, a feeling he remembered from fighting the Japanese on Guam. Boots squishing, he approached the building and for an instant lit the Zippo. Facing him was a door about four feet wide, held shut by a heavy oak bar running through metal straps but not in any way locked (for the risk of anyone stealing ice in Maine on a frosty night in September 1946 was at worst minimal). So when Greenleaf reached out through the dark and experimentally hefted the bar, it slid easily. He pulled the door open. Inside, flickering light from the lighter revealed a low, canvas-covered mass pushed against the back wall, the last of Ewen's 1946 harvest. About an inch of water covered the floor, and everywhere small piles of dunnage—sawdust and hay used for insulation—rose from the surface like tiny reefs and islands. Close to the door lay a pile of soggy burlap bags.

Back outside he stood on a loading platform and looked with the flickering light low along the wall; there he could discern another pile of burlap, larger than the one inside, and dry. He snapped the Zippo closed. In the dark he went back to the canoe, returned with the can, and sloshed gasoline over the burlap and against the wall. Gracefully, almost indifferently, he bent to the reeking bags with his small torch; the pile burst at once into a bright flare, and he stepped back quickly with a face blood red in the sudden incandescence. He slipped the Zippo into his pocket, picked up the gas can, and returned to the canoe. As he started paddling down the pond, he heard the burning wood crackle and saw his shadow dance crazily across the black water.

Behind him the fire was running hungry fingers up the wall, and when the sawdust insulation began to cascade onto the platform, the flames leaped twenty feet above the roof. The fire roared and shook, and the whole building was aflame, spewing sparks to the stars in a wild combustion of thousands of feet of dry pine and five or so cubic yards of sawdust. Greenleaf did not even look back.

Keeping close to the shore, he slipped quietly along, the glowing sky at his back. Ahead he heard the church bell ringing and men shouting at Cooper's Mills. The volunteer fire department was waking up. Ahead also he could hear a steady rush of water. He was approaching the Long Pond dam.

Actually there were two dams coming up, a small two-foot drop at the end of the pond and, two hundred yards farther, one eighteen or twenty feet high, which a century before had powered the wheel that gave Cooper's Mills its name. He knew both dams fairly well, but the last time he'd been over them had been in broad daylight, and then he'd had two hands. By starlight he saw the straight line of water, attacked it head on, and slid easily and swiftly over into the dark stream running down to the dark pool he could barely perceive through the crisp night, quick slip now (ah!) and into the eddy there; straightening and moving to the spillway on the right-hand side of the dam, the canoe hesitating, and then over the lip and falling fast and twisting, a wrench with the oar hard against the handless arm, arrow-straight down into the black night, diamond flashes on the water, scraped and shot through—under the bridge, into the smooth open pool, and slower, slower, stop: he took a breath.

"Well, Jesus," he whispered, and then swung the oar. The bow jumped ahead, downstream.

The river wound along for approximately ten miles to Whitefield in a series of shallow runs and deeper pools like pearls on a necklace. It never widened to more than twenty-five feet across, although its current ran swiftly enough. Still, the night for a time slowed Greenleaf's progress, for he could barely make out the river's course, much less see how deep the water was. Whenever he felt the canoe grounding in shallows, he had to hop out and, while holding onto a thwart, lower it to a deeper level. He had not gone more than a mile downstream in this fashion, shivering from wet and cold (though he was as oblivious of his discomfort as a tree in the rain), when the first glimmerings of dawn made it possible for him to shoot safely a short run of bumpy water without disembarking. Two miles beyond as he rounded a wide, quiet bend, he was able to see quite clearly the ancient Crossman ice house tottering beneath some pines on the east bank.

There were no Crossmans on the Sheepscot anymore, though their ghosts were prominent among those hanging like mist over the river. The original had been a successful criminal lawyer from Boston who in 1837 acquired for five hundred dollars a thousand-acre tract and seven years later ordered an architect named Thomas Pratt to design "a large house, a barn with carriage house, and various necessary outbuildings to be erected on my property in Maine. Further, I direct that the house shall contain two parlors, a dining room, kitchen and pantry, at least five bedrooms, servants' quarters, and whatever innovations you can otherwise devise." The plans were drawn and approved, and construction was begun in 1846. Five years later the Crossman estate was complete.

In 1855 he retired from practice and moved his wife and possessions to the farm, having invested his personal fortune discreetly and carefully in seven munitions companies throughout the north (a man would have to have been blind not to see the oncoming conflict; and it was said of Rufus Crossman that he could walk into a pitch-black orchard and come out with his pockets full of ripe apples, and not a wormy one in the lot, either). A year after the war at the age of seventy-five he found himself worth more than a million dollars. Then, two years later, he died.

Amazingly enough, his widow remained at the estate—amazingly because she at forty-one was still young and wealthy enough to be expected to return to Boston and reenter society. Nonetheless she did not. She may have been afraid of returning too close to the sources of her husband's fortune; for, as a criminal lawyer and a warmonger to boot, he must have had a few connections that were more than somewhat shady. It may, of course, have been her love for the Sheepscot region that kept her there, but whatever the cause, she stayed on in the decaying mansion until her death in 1905, when she joined her husband in the family graveyard. As a boy, Eustis Greenleaf had often seen her, a proud, still-beautiful woman in her seventies, being driven to Wiscasset in a horse-drawn carriage. Since her death the great empty house had fallen into ruins.

Greenleaf landed the canoe and went up to the ice house. Its roof had partially collapsed inward, as if from the weight of the pine needles covering it. The walls were tinged green with moss, and there was no door. A red squirrel chattered angrily at him. He stood at the doorway, reached up with the cigarette lighter like the Statue of Liberty, and lit the needles on the roof. As he stepped back, the flames dashed up to the peak, snapping and spitting sparks through the broken boards onto the needle-covered floor below. Soon the old building was completely afire. The damp, rotten wood burned neither sharply nor cleanly, but sent billowing clouds of smoke into the sky.

Dawn was upon him. At this point he was only four miles from his father's house. For seven miles, as far down as Whitefield, he was completely familiar with each rock and run, with each pool and shallow, with each building on each shore, with each element and its arrangement that constituted this stretch of the river. So he knew for a certainty there was only one ice house between the Crossman estate and the old King's Mill dam at Whitefield, and he knew precisely where it sat—on the west bank directly across from a path which led from the river a half-mile through the woods to the back door of his father's house.

Ahead he saw the North Whitefield bridge approaching. As the canoe slipped easily beneath it, an elderly man leaned over the railing and waved to him. "That you, Alcott?"

He hunched in the boat, trying to protect his face and the stump of his wrist from view; and the old man did not call again. (Greenleaf knew him all right, a retired farmer named Walton Northey. Walton had the reputation of being as sharp-eyed as an osprey. On fine fall mornings he often took his breechloading twenty-gauge Winchester for a walk in the woods. He carried only two shells, one in each barrel, and he rarely returned without a brace of birds. There was a story that someone had once met him coming home with three, a woodcock and two partridge.

"How'd you get the three, Walton? Thought you never took more than two shots."

"Ayuh," he had said. "Well, I shot the cock first, don't you know. Then I come up on the partridges about ten feet apart, feeding. They was a rock between 'em, so I aimed at that and split the charge.")

Greenleaf did not look back at the bridge. "Old bastid," he said bitterly to himself. He felt rage and despair wash through him again, not so much because he had been seen and recognized, but mostly because he was so close to home. His paddling became erratic, and the canoe banged unnecessarily against a rock. When it grounded at a shallow run, he bounded from it furiously, pulling and jerking it over the stones, punctuating each movement with a squeak from his throat. Finally he rounded the bend in the river where the ice house stood; he rammed the canoe against the shore and jumped out.

In the fall of 1915 Eustis Greenleaf had built this ice house for his friend Horace Barker, a dairy farmer. He was then twenty-three, working on the house crew of the Tidewater Ice Company in Wiscasset. In January of 1916 Tidewater's steam generator powering the elevator that lifted the hundred-pound cakes of ice up to the runs exploded, some said because (but this was never proved) an engineer named Buster Racine wedged a timber between the boiler's blow-off valve and the ceiling in order to produce more lift. No matter why; it remained that Eustis's right leg was severed at the knee by a piece of flying iron plate, and his days in the great house were abruptly ended. Horace Barker, who had not yet settled with him for the work on the ice house, offered him twenty acres of land on the Whitefield Road as payment. It was the only bit of charity Eustis would allow himself, except that when the Tidewater Ice Company offered to pay his medical expenses and a small compensation, he grimly accepted.

Here thirty years later Greenleaf stalked toward the building. Even now it was in good shape, having been refloored several times (twice by Eustis himself, leg or no leg). He opened the door and saw that the room was empty and swept clean, a strange condition for this time of year, for even if Barker had run out of ice, he would still buy a couple hundred pounds more to guard against Indian summer. But the house did not look as if it had been used at all this season. (In fact it had not; in this year of 1946, with electricity available to rural subscribers for nearly thirty years, Horace Barker had at last decided to keep his milk and butter cool with the help of the Frigidaire and the Central Maine Power companies.)

So this time there was no tinder, but the room was bone dry. He ran back to the canoe for the gasoline. Sloshing about a cupful at the corner of the door frame, he held the cigarette lighter there and flicked it; there was a gentle puff of fire. He stood up and moved back, watching the nearly invisible flames begin to eat at the gray wood. At his back the sun rose slow and red, and thus fires grew both before and behind him while he stood silent now and straight, new tears staining his erect and strained face.

Then came a swishing implosion as oxygen rushed in to feed newly released sawdust in combustive urgency, followed by the *whump!* of the explosion, soft but massive in his face; and his tears gradually stopped and dried upon his cheeks. For the first time he stood watching the fire burn, rage, and roar; listening to the cracks and snaps; smelling the sweet scent of burning pine. He looked up at the sky, saw the white pillar of smoke beaconing in the clear morning, and hurried to the canoe.

The river moved, and Greenleaf with it, without obstruction for four miles to Whitefield. Halfway there he could hear bells ringing, the distant clamor of the town's alarm; and when he came boiling under the bridge, what he could see of Whitefield was deserted. He climbed out at the old spillway of the King's Mill dam and, holding onto the canoe's stern, allowed it to lead him down, scraping past jutting rocks and over small falls. Once he tripped forward and fell in nearly to his waist, but he was up quickly, getting his feet out in front of him again to catch the rocks the way a mountaineer rappels down a cliff face. At the bottom, back in the canoe, he took the lighter from his pocket. Water had not penetrated to the wick, which lit easily. He put it in the breast pocket of his khaki shirt and buttoned the flap.

Four miles downstream on the east bank was an ice house owned by a farmer named Sibley Tukey. Greenleaf knew the building, knew Tukey by reputation: tall and gaunt, widowed twice and recently married a third time, a man of whom it was said that he could squeeze a nickel so hard that the buffalo on the back would be wrung dry. Tukey's well-known distrust of banks had been justified in 1929 (a fact of which he never tired of reminding his neighbors), and rumors of socks full of gold stuffed in his mattress or silver hidden under his hearth had circulated widely enough anyway for him to have gathered three successive wives to his thin breast.

The ice house lay about seventy yards from the main one, well within its view. Greenleaf knew that the old man would probably have been up working for some time now, so he kept close to the east shore as he drew past Tukey's place—a neat, drab arrangement of buildings and fields, the ice house sheltered by a huge maple, the leaves of which were already growing dark in expectation of autumn. A hundred yards beyond the farm, under a birch-shrouded bank, he beached the canoe.

He carried what was left of his gasoline with him, moving quickly and carefully along the shore, keeping low behind the shrubs that lined it. A ramp had been cut through the bank from the ice house to the river, a distance of perhaps forty feet. From a crouch he peered about and listened, but could see and hear no evidence of the old man's presence. Just as he was about to make a run for it, a high thin shriek of laughter floated from the main house toward him: "Damn you, Sibley, cut it out! Get along and leave me alone!"

With the can tucked under his handless arm, Greenleaf ran up the ramp to the ice house, went cautiously around the side to the door, opened it, and entered, pulling it nearly but not entirely closed behind him. Dimly visible were masses of ice against the back wall and heaps of sawdust soggy in the water that covered the floor. He peeked out the doorway and, perceiving no sign of Tukey in his amorousness, darted out and around the building.

He sloshed gasoline against the back wall and flipped the empty can into the river. From his pocket came once more the trusty Zippo, which sent sudden flames shooting up the side of the ice house. Then he dashed through the river to the canoe where he sat listening, his head cocked in intensity like a robin straining for the frail subterranean rumble of an earthworm. He heard nothing, however; the river was babbling too brightly for him to pick up the crackling of burning wood. At last he saw the smoke and was about to proceed when a distant voice roaring in rage made him hesitate: "Goddamnit, Elizabeth! Fire!"

Only then did he push off, leaving Tukey's anger to join the ashes of both ice house and lust.

Sunlight danced over the water as he rammed the canoe purposefully downstream. The day would be bright and warm, he saw, a gift from a dying summer, but he was not cheered or otherwise affected by this. Like a vessel of dark oils, he had become filled with a grim satisfaction that had nothing to do with the weather. Passing several houses, he came finally to a point where he could see the church spire at Head Tide rising over the trees ahead. Here was the last dam on the river; seven miles below it stood the next ice house. He entered the dam pond and paddled to the east side where he could see the sluice gate, a four-foot-square opening in the concrete through which the river's waters incessantly spewed. They then struck a huge boulder of granite cropping out from the bank, which deflected them back toward the middle of the riverbed.

As he entered the sluice gate, he ducked his head. The canoe hesitated at the lip and darted over; he backed water to turn to the right, away from the granite, but could not generate power against the water's rush; the canoe, angled slightly toward shore, hurtled at the boulder; lacking a left hand, he could not paddle from that side and so hesitated, then tried to flip the stern to the left, drove the oar down, twisted and pulled with his crooked and handless arm to see the oar snap from his fingers; the bow struck the boulder with the sound of splintering wood, and the stern rose from the water, and the whole canoe stood vertically for an instant; seeing everything (the sky above, the water below, the rocks to all sides) poised, already separating from the fractured canoe, he shouted in dismay and fury, "Oh you bastid!" And fell: through air and water and mist into the pool below.

After the splash had settled back into the surface, his head popped out from it. Slowly he swam to shore and climbed out.

2

UNDER normal circumstances Sheriff Bartholomew Ware would spend a reasonable amount of Sunday morning in bed. He would get up around eight thirty and take an hour or so with breakfast and the Downeast edition of the Portland Sunday *Telegram* before beginning the day. Most Sundays he never even went down to the office at all, an omission that affected no one, for the telephone operators knew enough to route any off-hour emergency to his house. Above all the sheriff was a reasonable man, and although he did not attend church, he felt with his soul that the voters of Lincoln County had not elected him to his post expecting him to be in his office at seven thirty on the morning of the Lord's own day.

However, on Sunday, September 1, 1946, Labor Day weekend intruded upon the sanctity of the Lord's designated rest and coincidentally upon the sheriff's as well. An unflagging sense of responsibility (aided by his alarm clock) drove the sheriff from his bed at six thirty.

"Hell's bells." He rolled over and slapped off the alarm.

His wife, Emily, opened one eye. "You want me to make you breakfast?"

"Uhuh, Emmy. I'll get her." And saw her instantly shut the eye.

In his pajamas he went first to the kitchen, where he set both a kettle and a saucepan of water on the stove to boil. He then strode back through the bedroom into the bathroom, with each step growing more decisive. When he reentered the kitchen—shaved and cleaned and uniformed—he was fully awake and the water in both pots was boiling excitedly.

His breakfast was invariable: a bowl of Shredded Wheat, an egg boiled so soft that the white looked like a bit of clear jellyfish, two pieces of toasted homemade bread, and a mug of black tea. The menu was a legacy from his father, who himself began each day with the same meal (except for the Shredded Wheat) until he died at eighty-seven. A pretty good track record, the sheriff thought, whenever he thought anything about it.

He brought in the *Telegram* and set it on the table. Then he got a bowl and put into it a Shredded Wheat biscuit. The Nabisco people had recently begun printing pictures of Straight Arrow on the cards that separated the tiers of biscuits, and Emily was saving them at the request of the paper boy. Removing a card that described some arcane snatches of trail-finding lore, he placed it on the sill above the sink. It was too bad, he mused while spooning the egg gently into the saucepan, that he and Em had never had children. (It was a familiar thought. In the darkness of their bed, Emily asleep beside him, he occasionally wondered at the source of their sterility, whether it hid somewhere deep inside her soft and inscrutable body, the female organism which beneath its calm surface churned in endless cycles and rhythms; or whether the fault lay in himself, a weakness perhaps from wearing his reproductive organs on his sleeve, so to speak—for how could he protect something he could not contain within him?—but he could never say, and for shame or fear would never go to a doctor to find out.) He sat down to eat.

Looking first at the sports page, he saw that the Red Sox had beaten the Athletics and the Yankees the Senators both by a score of four–two and were due to play again this afternoon in Philadelphia and Washington, respectively. The standings were not affected, since both teams won: Boston was still in first place by thirteen and a half games. He next turned to the comic section and read "Orphan Annie" and "Dick Tracy." Annie and Sandy had finally discovered that the mysterious Lotus, for weeks believed to be a beautiful native girl, was in fact a monkey. The sheriff was delighted. Dick Tracy had met up with a female disk jockey named Christmas Early as she choked a man whose head was trapped in a revolving door through which she was trying to pass. For years Sheriff Ware had read "Dick Tracy" with fascination. When Diet Smith had presented Dick with the two-way wrist radio the previous January, he became so excited that he wrote to Chester Gould, the author of the strip, to ask if there was a factual basis for the device. He had received a brief but courteous reply from Gould that there was not.

The telephone rang. He got to it quickly to avoid waking his wife. "Hello?"

"That you, Sheriff?"

"Ayuh."

"Say, this is Frank Ewen up to Cooper's Mills. Hope I didn't wake you up."

"Not a bit, Frank. Been up an hour. What's the matter? Trouble?"

"Some. We had a couple of fires up here this morning. Both ice houses on Long Pond—mine and Gussie Prescott's. Burned flat."

"Goddamn. You say *both?*"

"Ayuh. Mine burned so goddamned fast it left the ice unmelted in the middle of the floor."

"What time?"

"Well, the alarm sounded about three thirty, quarter to four. That was for mine. Prescott's was already ashes. We was some lucky the woods didn't go up."

Sheriff Ware was silent for a few seconds. "Huh. Probably some of them damn kids. Well, look, Frank, I'll be up there in half, three quarters of an hour. I got to set up today's traffic details, and afterwards I'll be right along."

"Thanks. Be seeing you."

He went out to his Nash. The lawn sparkled with dew in the sunshine, and in the shadow cast by the hedge, faint signs of last night's frost—first of the fall—tinged the grass white. Despite the cold night the Nash burst into immediate and cheerful combustion. After warming it up for a couple of minutes, he backed out of his driveway and headed up the hill toward town. It was then five minutes to seven.

His office was located in the basement of the Lincoln County Courthouse, the oldest functioning courthouse in Maine. Begun in 1818 and completed six years later by a man with the unlikely name of Tileston Cushing, it had since then perched on the hill at the head of Main Street overlooking the town like a huge square brick-and-granite eagle. (Still, despite its venerability, the structure marked the end rather than the beginning of Wiscasset's golden age. In the eighteenth century the town had been an important shipping community, a port of entry where the likes of Talleyrand and

Louis Philippe first entered the Commonwealth of Massachusetts and thus the United States of America. By the time the courthouse was built, however, the town found itself unmoored—the Embargo Act of 1807 and the War of 1812 had removed its port-of-entry status; the Compromise of 1820 had removed it from Massachusetts—and the stately building was left to the quiet business of administering justice for a county that possessed three towns with populations greater than one thousand people and none with more than five.) The sheriff parked in his slot in the rear of the building, beside Deputy Sheriff Ed Leeman's Ford, both vehicles starred, antennaed, and marked "L.C.S.D."

Entering the office, he nodded with approval to his deputy. "Morning, Ed. Up early, eh?"

"Naw, Bee. Just got here."

"Nice day."

"Cold night, though. Frost got Hazel's tomatoes."

"Ayuh."

Leeman at twenty-four was tall and good looking, with large white teeth and brown eyes, and inordinately stupid. The sheriff was fond of him but well aware of his limitations. "You know, Ed's a real nice fellow," he once remarked to his wife, "but he couldn't pour skim milk out of a rubber boot with the directions printed on the heel." Still, he had a reputation for being honest and faithful and brave and willing; when he had returned from World War II with a Purple Heart, the sheriff had been glad to offer him a deputy's badge. It was only necessary to explain everything to him very carefully.

"Ed, I got to go up to Long Pond this morning. There was a couple of ice houses that burned down there last night. They seem to think they was set. Why don't you check with the state and see what areas they figure they might need traffic help with. Then get in touch with Eldridge Billings in Waldoboro if you're going to want him. He's on call today."

"Sure, Bee. Think you got a firebug on your hands?"

"Can't say. Frank Ewen called me this morning. He was pretty excited."

"Right."

"Now, Ed, check with Emmy every once in a while. If there's any trouble, she'll get the messages. If you need me, you can try the radio. I'll keep it on. It hasn't been working much lately, but if you shout loud enough, I might be able to hear you."

"Right."

The telephone rang; the deputy picked it up. "Sheriff's Office, Deputy Leeman. Oh, hi, Em. Want to talk to the boss?"

He handed the receiver to Ware, who said, "Ayuh?" and then listened. Finally, "Okay, Emmy, thanks. I'll be heading up there right off. Oh, you want to hold any messages for Ed or me? Ayuh, good. Okay." He hung up.

"What's up?"

"She got a call from Whitefield right after I left the house. They just had a fire alarm from a farmer named Horace Barker. Another ice house. We'll see you, Ed. Keep your fly buttoned." In the sheriff's wake Deputy Leeman blinked, remembered his assignment, snapped shut his mouth, and went to the telephone to call the State Police and Eldridge Billings.

By nine o'clock Sheriff Ware possessed all but the most crucial facts of his case: he knew that someone had set four ice houses afire—Prescott's, Ewen's, Crossman's, and Barker's—between the hours of one and seven thirty that morning; that whoever had done it had apparently first wrecked an unregistered and mongrelized Model A pickup on the Long

Pond road and then stolen a canoe, fashioning a paddle for it by burning an oar in half; that each ice house was approached from the water; even that whoever was setting the fires wore size eight boots with badly worn soles and heels, most of the wear occurring on the outside of the boots. He did not know that Walton Northey had seen someone who he thought was Alcott Greenleaf come barreling under the North Whitefield bridge at about six thirty (but he would soon; news traveled quickly along the river). Coincidentally, the Greenleaf name had been mentioned to the sheriff in the course of the morning, when Frank Ewen happened to mention that the old man, Eustis, had bought fifty pounds of ice from him the day before. But at this point the card with young Alcott's name had not been dealt into the sheriff's hand. Thus, he was able to deduce only that the arsonist was light in weight, pigeon-toed, and well acquainted with the area, and that it would behoove him (the sheriff) to find the next ice house downriver before it too joined its brothers in flames.

Standing beside Barker, surveying the still-smoking ruins, he asked, "Horace, who else has an ice house around here?"

"Well, Sheriff, I'm not sure. As far as I know, there's nothing down to Whitefield. A year ago, before I switched to electricity, I was shopping for some ice to tide me over till winter. I had a hell of a time. Frank Ewen was out. I finally got some from an old baster down to Head Tide named Sibley Tukey."

"Jesus. I know Sibley. I bet that ice came dear."

"I don't know about that." He paused. "If it was a solid piece of diamond, you would have said I got a real good deal on it."

"Ayuh. Ha. Sibley got a phone, you think?"

"He didn't last year. Too tight."

"Ayuh. Look, Horace, I'll be back to you later."

"Sure thing, Sheriff."

And with celerity he departed: stones flying from under the wheels of the Nash, speedometer hovering like a hummingbird at sixty, siren screaming through the clean September morning. He crossed the Whitefield bridge, continuing down the river. With the rattle of rocks beneath the floorboards he whipped the Nash onto Tukey's dirt road less than fifteen minutes after he left Barker's. Ahead he saw wisps of smoke still rising. "Goddamn," he said to himself, shutting off the siren and stopping in front of the house.

As he got out of the car and walked around to the back, he could hear the old man's tenor voice, strong and clear, railing at his wife, the pair of them returning to the house: "Goddamnit all, Elizabeth, that fire didn't start all by itself! And if I ever catch the miserable son of a bitch who done it, I'll kick him so hard the snot will come leaking right through his sneakers! Probably one of them goddamn kids—" The sheriff was suddenly standing in the path before them.

"Sheriff! Goddamnit, somebody just burned my ice house."

"Don't shout, Sibley. I know it. That's why I'm here."

"You know it?" Sibley shrieked, jerking and bobbing and frothing as if in seizure. "How in the sambilly hell do you know somebody burned my ice house?" The old man's fists were clenched, and tears of rage shook in his eyes. Beside him, his wife stood arrested in the presence of such passion (he seemed at the threshold of a coronary, and God alone knew or even could have guessed at the whirlpool of emotions swirling through her—lusty bride, helpmate, spectator, heiress).

"Now, quiet down, Sibley. That kind of attitude ain't going to help. I know it was burned because four other ice houses upriver were burned this morning along with it.

There's a firebug going right down the Sheepscot in a canoe."

"Well, goddamnit—"

"Now, just relax. Whoever it is can't be too far away by now, even with the river helping him. Where's the next ice house? Maybe I can get to that one before he does."

Calming, he replied, "Well, downriver—let me see now—there's only one more that I know about. Francis Wiggins, down by Sheepscot. But damn it all, Sheriff—"

"Thanks, Sibley. Someone will check back with you later."

As the sheriff turned to go, the wife tugged at her husband's sleeve. He bent his ear to her mouth. The sheriff could not hear her whisper, but even when he had slid inside the car, he could still hear Tukey's roaring: "No, we *ain't* going to get a goddamned refrigerator, Elizabeth! I ain't spending all that money to get electricity in here! Now, wipe the soot and the snot off your face and get into that house, goddamnit—"

After the sheriff started the Nash and rolled up the windows, the old man's rantings were faint. As he drove away, they died from his ears altogether.

3

THE early afternoon sun was warm as it filtered through the leaves onto Greenleaf's back. From the thicket in which he lay he could hear only faint murmurings: the river slipping gracefully over and among the rocks; those crickets and flies that had survived last night's frost distantly chirping and buzzing; and the two men that stood talking beside the ice house. He watched the men carefully: one tall and bony, dressed in overalls and a blue work shirt; the other older, heavier, wearing the beige uniform of a county sheriff. He wished he could make out what they were talking about, but he did not dare approach nearer.

After his fall into the river, he had pulled himself out onto the west bank. There he stripped, wrung out his clothes, and stretched them over some bushes to dry. He discovered that the Zippo had fallen out of his breast pocket, a loss that at first angered him; but he consoled himself by remembering those unsolicited testimonials in *Field and Stream* from lucky men who recovered their long-lost Zippos still operable from the bellies of trout. Be a hell of a big fish, he thought. Lying nude in the sunshine, he dozed comfortably and dreamed of huge fish with distended stomachs which, when cut open, revealed jewels and precious metals, flashing like flames as they dropped into his hands.

When he woke, he put on his still-damp clothes, scrambled up the embankment to the road, and began walking south toward Wiscasset. Alna was less than two miles away. Before he had covered half that distance, he saw a Flying A sign leaning out over the road ahead, which proved to be the marker for the gasoline pump at Tomkins's Variety Store.

He stepped into the store, letting the screen door slap behind him. It was dark and cool inside, the floor gray and unvarnished with occasional glintings of nails worn shiny. To his right as he entered was a glass candy case, and behind it stood a woman he did not know—short, wrinkled, wearing gold-rimmed spectacles and a shapeless cotton dress.

"Morning, young fellow."

"Ayuh. Pretty one."

"It sure is. What can I do for you?"

"Pack of Luckies."

She handed him the cigarettes and a book of matches.

"Got a can of lighter fluid?"

"I suppose so." She turned around and shuffled toward the back, still talking over her shoulder. "Say. You heard anything about these fires? The ones along the river?"

"Some. I hear they caught the man who done it. I was

talking to a fisherman down on the river, and he said they got him."

"Good." She brought back a can of lighter fluid and set it on the counter. "That'll be sixty-two cents." He took his wallet from his hip pocket and handed her a dollar bill. "Why, your money's damp."

"Ayuh. I fell in the river."

"I bet it was cold," she said, handing him his change.

Then he walked the six miles to Wiggins's farm, where stood the only other ice house on the river above Wiscasset that he knew anything about. Francis Wiggins was twenty-eight, the only son of a never prosperous farmer who had barely managed to hold onto his land during the Depression and who afterward broke his back to allow his boy to attend the University of Maine in Orono. Francis—tall, gangling, large handed, infinitely serious about his studies—could run as fast as a spooked deer, though without its grace. There were a few football scholarships available, he had discovered with disbelief ("You mean they pay you to play that shit-ass game?"), and he tried out for the team, never before having touched a ball. But he could run, and his big hands could hold onto a pass, so they tried him at end. When no one on the team could catch him, let alone wrestle him down, the excited coach offered him tuition, books, and room and board if he would play for the team. At the end of his first season he had caught seventeen passes for touchdowns. He continued to hate the game, but continued to play it anyway until the first scrimmage of his senior year, when a broken leg concluded the gratuitous nature of his education.

By this time his father was able to help him finish, although not without difficulty. Graduating in June of 1942, he enlisted in the Army and served as a medic at Pearl Harbor, where briefly—small world and marvelous!—he encountered Alcott Greenleaf handless and feverish in an Army hospital. Two months after Wiggins returned in 1945, his father died of an aneurysm, leaving him equipped with Army experience and a university degree to raise the farm from its bed of poverty. In the past year he had made a little headway.

Greenleaf had smoked his Luckies most of the way, feeling almost joyful, humming to himself while he walked along. (Once on Guam his platoon had been deployed on a reconnaissance mission over nearly six miles of jungle trails. Three miles out, one of their number was shot in the neck by a Japanese sniper. Greenleaf spotted the sniper's position, circled with extreme care, and killed him with one shot from his rifle. Then his fear and rage and hatred underwent this same joyous transformation. Despite the stealth with which he was forced to travel, he quietly hummed and sang his way through most of the remainder of the mission. He returned successfully, but three weeks later his left hand was blown off at the wrist.)

At last he approached the Wiggins ice house from the woods and, seeing the farmer sitting beside it, dropped silently into a thick copse of alders about fifty yards away. After fifteen minutes the sheriff had come, and the two men had been talking for nearly ten more. Now he dozed, washed in the soft warm breeze.

Suddenly the sheriff's voice brought him awake. "Goddamnit, Francis! Look at that!"

They ran toward the river. From his position Greenleaf could not see what the sheriff was pointing at. He watched as he stripped off his uniform, dived into the water, and swam out of view. When he came splashing back, he was pushing ahead of him the broken bow section of the canoe.

On the shore the men talked animatedly. The sheriff

picked up his clothes, the farmer the piece of canoe, and they walked together up to the farmhouse. The instant the door closed behind them, Greenleaf, keeping low to the ground, scuttled like a crab across the open field to the ice house. He opened the door and jumped inside, leaving it cracked ajar to admit a single knife-edge of light.

The floor was only slightly damp, the room empty and clean. He leaned against the wall, catching his breath and letting his eyes adjust to the dimness while he listened for any sounds of discovery from either Wiggins or the sheriff. There were none.

By the door leaned a two-pronged iron busting bar, a crowbarlike tool used both to pry off cakes during ice harvest and to break apart those frozen together in storage. He seized it and walked around the interior of the room, poking at the lower wall boards. One, rotted by summers of dampness, gave slightly at his touch; he raised the bar and drove it through like a spear. Sawdust cascaded out of the hole onto the floor.

Methodically he doused the sawdust with lighter fluid and then put a cigarette in his mouth. Next he lit a match by bending it in half while still in the book and scraping it with his thumb across the emery paper. It flared brightly in the dim room until he sucked the cigarette alive and, exhaling, blew the room black again. Finally in the reeking sawdust he stood the smoldering cigarette as erect as a fence post, packing a solid base around it. If it don't work, he thought, it don't work, but I can't sit around and wait to find out. He had always hated school, had hated all the indignities it had forced upon him, and even six years later could not remember it with anything close to pleasure; but for some reason now he dredged up the last lines of a poem he had once been forced to memorize for recitation—"For I have promises to keep, and miles to go before I sleep."

He giggled. Miles to go before I sleep. That was the ticket. Closing the door behind him, he stepped from the ice house and darted into the woods.

4

WHEN Sheriff Ware walked with Francis Wiggins back to the farmhouse to get dressed, he was feeling pleased. Running a towel over his body, he said, "I'll tell you, Francis, this piece of canoe explains plenty. I couldn't figure what happened to our friend, but he must have cracked up along the river someplace. Look, let me use your phone. My radio is buzzing worse than a bee in a bottle. I want to call my wife and have her get hold of my deputy. He and I can work up the river and see if we can find out where our boy came a cropper."

"Sure, Sheriff."

"Thanks." He put on his pants and took up the telephone. "Ayuh," he said into it, "give me 7-7-7-0. Hello, Emmy? Any calls? Ayuh. . . . Who? The junkman? Ayuh, I know him." He paused. "What's Ed doing? Ayuh, that means he ain't doing a damned thing. When he calls in again, tell him to get up here to the Wiggins farm in Sheepscot. Meanwhile, I'll go check out the Greenleafs. Okay. Bye."

He hung up, then instantly picked up the receiver again. "Ayuh. Get me Eustis Greenleaf in Whitefield." There was a long pause. "All right. Thanks anyway."

He turned back to Wiggins, buttoning his shirt. "An old fellow named Walton Northey in North Whitefield thinks he saw Alcott Greenleaf canoeing downriver about six o'clock this morning."

"That right? I know Alcott. Met him in a Pearl Harbor hospital after he had his hand blown off. Funny thing. He lives ten miles from here and I never knew him before and I haven't seen him since. But I met him just one time, halfway round the world."

"Damned strange," agreed the sheriff, "but I think Walton Northey seeing him on the river this morning is even stranger."

The two men walked to the front door. "I'm headed up to Greenleaf's now. When my deputy, Ed Leeman, gets here, tell him to watch the ice house. In the meantime, maybe you ought to keep an eye on it yourself."

"Sure thing, Sheriff. I will. In fact—" There was a soft dull rushing sound, like a haystack being dropped on a barn floor.

"Goddamnit," said the sheriff, who saw the smoke suddenly rise from behind the house.

"Anyway, I guess he didn't get drowned when his canoe broke up," said Wiggins.

By the time they got the fire out, the building had been reduced to ashes and dust. The sheriff, who had reached an emotional stage where he took thwarting of his shrieval activities as a personal affront, furiously assumed all responsibility for its loss. "Jesus, Francis, I'm sorry. It's my own goddamned fault. If it's that Greenleaf kid, I'll slap the little clown black and blue."

"Relax, Sheriff. It wasn't your fault. You'll get him."

The sheriff wiped a sooty hand across his sooty forehead. "Ayuh. We will. You can bet on it."

"What's up, Bee? Another fire?" They turned to face Deputy Leeman's interested brown eyes.

"Hah? Oh. Ayuh, that's it all right."

"Catch the firebug?"

"Nope. Not yet." The sheriff spoke slowly. "Look, I want you to go down the river the rest of the way to Wiscasset and find out if anybody's got an ice house. Check both sides of the river. If they do, tell them to stick to it as tight as a tick. Then call Emmy and tell her how you made out. She'll tell you what next. Got it?"

The deputy nodded. "You bet."

"I got to get up to Greenleaf's." He strode purposefully toward the Nash.

"Sheriff," said Wiggins.

"Ayuh?"

"Maybe you'd like to wash your face and hands before you go."

"Oh. Ayuh."

The sheriff discovered a blister on the heel of his right hand and several other burns elsewhere. While he drove the ten miles to Greenleaf's they throbbed, mute echoes of his raging and aching soul. It was not right, he mused, that Eustis Greenleaf's boy, to whom he had never even spoken harshly, much less done injury, should cause him such discomfort. (By now he was definite in his mind that it was Alcott he sought. The possibility that old Northey had been mistaken in identifying him was too painful to bear, for it left the sheriff with six counts of arson and nary a suspect to match against any one of them.)

He knew Eustis slightly from the old days. After the boiler blew his leg off, he had demanded it returned to him; and the sheriff had seen it at the house, fleshless of course and bleached white, wired together and hung over the wood stove like a stag rack—tibia, fibula, tarsals, metatarsals, heel, and toes. Remembering this morbid sight, the sheriff's anger became tinged with a vague foreboding. Then he rounded a curve and suddenly was there.

A big sign stood by the road, had stood there for the past fifteen years: SCRAP METALS, USED AUTO PARTS, BOUGHT AND SOLD. E. GREENLEAF & SON. Beyond it, defining the driveway the way a lawn would, lay every form of metal scrap conceivable: broken fenders and chassis, stoves, washing machines, and iceboxes; empty metal barrels, barrels full of nuts, bolts, washers, and wires; bedsprings, aircraft wings, hoops, fencing material—all rusting in injured noiselessness, decaying helplessly, a vast graveyard for white elephants.

At the right of the house itself was blocked a big blue Pontiac, facing the road with a shattered and dented front end. Painted across the side in foot-high letters was LOSE LIPS SINK SHIPS! REMEBER PEARL HBR! Thus it had lain since Eustis had put it there in 1943, a memorial to his son's enlistment. The sheriff parked nose-to-nose with this moribund automobile and with quick steps went to the door to knock. The subsequent silence was profound.

"Eustis?" he called. Still no sound.

He pulled the screen open and turned the knob. The door opened quietly and easily, and he stepped inside.

His first impression upon entering was visual, one of great clutter. It was as if all the furniture in the house (and indeed Eustis had gathered together many discarded bureaus, chairs, tables, and lamps in his day) had been moved into the front room. Such a jumbled assortment of objects testified to much activity, to much scurrying and carrying, but still the house stood in its profound silence. His second impression served to augment the profundity of this quietness, for he felt a cold and oppressive dankness permeating the house. Despite the sunshine spilling through the windows, the sheriff felt as though he had stepped into a dark cellar, or a morgue.

He had entered into the wide front room of the house. To his left was the kitchen; before him past the furniture were two bedroom doors. Both were open. Through one he could see an unmade bed; through the other, nothing save for a worn, dark red, oriental-style rug. Against this door frame, complete with shoe and sock, leaned an artificial leg. Toward it he moved—slowly, dreadfully.

This inner room was absolutely bare of furniture. From a beam in the center, a foot above the floor, a body hung perfectly motionless, stiff and rigid as a side of beef in a freezer. The single leg was twisted in arrested agony. The sheriff's mind moved quickly from horror and shock to breaking suspicion and certainty. A man needs a scaffold for his hanging, he thought, especially if he's only got one leg to climb it with; and as he tugged a chair from the front room across the damp, dark rug, his heart was beating like muffled snares at an execution.

5

FOR the Tidewater Ice Company house in Wiscasset, mere existence was in 1946 miraculous. It was then the only large commercial ice house left in the state of Maine; every other had long ago burned down or rotted to dust. But Wiscasset is a town of this sort of miracle. Two wooden trading schooners—one still bearing the nameplate *Luther Little,* the other anonymous by now, its identity shrouded in the thick fog of time—ancient moldering hulls with a few spars still aloft, have lain for years against the west shore of the river there, lie there to this day—outlasting not only the lives of men who sailed them to Wiscasset but also the entire epoch of its history when it was vigorous and prosperous and young.

The Tidewater house stood on the north shore of Birch Cove, a deepwater inlet just south of the town. It was gargantuan: one hundred eighty feet long, thirty feet wide, and forty-seven feet high at gable peak, divided within into six thirty-foot-square rooms or storage areas, giving it a total capacity of twenty thousand tons of ice. In its day it had employed twenty-seven men, every one of whom prayed devoutly that the winter nights keep consistently below zero—and thereby keep him consistently at work—making the white gold that come summer would be shipped to New York and Philadelphia to cool juleps for those Manhattan and Chestnut Hill ladies who sat glowing in the oven of August. The ice was harvested from nearby ponds (the Sheepscot at Wiscasset was salt; unlike commercial sets on, say, the Kennebec, Tidewater could not use the ice that glistened tantalizingly fifteen feet from its south wall from December through March) and then transported to the house at first by sledge and finally by truck. By now that past may have receded too far to be easily recalled and appreciated: cold so hard that mucus froze in the nostrils, cracks of whips and groans of cold harness and wood, scrapings of sledge runners and horseshoe calks on ice and occasional stones, cries of men, fresh manure steaming in the white tracks as the great horses strained toward the great house. Or in summer the ice leaving Tidewater by ship from the south doors or by rail from the north ones, with the housemen breaking the hundred-pound cakes apart and driving them—legless, mindless cattle—along the runs to either the pier or the loading platform.

With the accident that cost Eustis his leg in 1916, Tidewater's operations ceased, as it turned out, for good. World War I intervened, and by 1920 the ice industry everywhere was through, over and done with. Because repairs had been instigated during the summer of 1916, the Tidewater set was in better shape than any other in Maine. This may be why it survived after the owners officially shut it down unused two years later. But also it was lucky: in the thirty years since the explosion, neither tramps nor boys nor town drunks nor anyone else had thrown burning cigarettes upon its floors or otherwise set it afire. The roof and sides were intact, as were most of the interior walls. Inside it was wide and empty, dry and dusty, on Labor Day Eve of 1946 when Alcott Greenleaf came to burn it down.

As the sun set, he was sitting along the shore beside a large elm perhaps two hundred yards from the building. He had been there for more than an hour, not moving, hidden by the tall brown grass like a duck hunter in a blind. He had seen the changing of the guard as Sheriff Ware replaced Deputy Leeman on stakeout. The Nash was parked as inconspicuously as possible behind some bushes that lined the Birch Point road. The road ran along a ridge below which was a big grassy field that swept down to the ice house. The two men and the building formed an isosceles right triangle: Greenleaf's side two hundred yards along the shore; the sheriff's also two hundred yards, but aimed directly toward the water; the hypotenuse between them running (granting the accuracy of the first two figures) two hundred eighty-three yards across the field.

After the sun had dropped below the horizon, Greenleaf moved. Crouching below the bank—the tide was down, affording him low rocks over which he could travel without being seen from the ridge above—he scampered toward the ice house. A large can hampered his flight. For the final twenty yards the bank was too low to hide him, forcing him to crawl through the grass on his elbows, commandolike, carefully pushing the can in front of him. When he finally reached the building, he stood up and dashed through one of the gaping doorways, over which was plastered one of the red-and-white *Keep Out! Trespassers Will Be Prosecuted!* signs that covered the walls, facing all directions, stern warnings toward both land and sea like flashings from a lighthouse.

He had been inside nearly five minutes when the sheriff

started the Nash. Greenleaf heard the engine's roar. The gathering darkness sheltered him as he leaped from the door he had entered, empty-handed now and hunched over at the waist, and hurried through the grass, aiming roughly at the midpoint of the hypotenuse (not at the point from which he had started, for he had no intention of escaping anyway), keeping his eye all the while upon the course of the Nash's lights as they pierced a way down the road toward a path leading onto the field. The bright beams swung jerkily over the dark and silent ice house and played across the grass where, motionless now and scarcely breathing, Greenleaf was squatting.

Suddenly he was up and running through the lights toward the building and the shore, almost in the direction he had just come from, nearly erect, a tightrope walker in the spotlights dashing to the safety of his platform. Then there was a shout, "Hold up! Stop!" and a tongue of orange fire lashed out with a roar. Greenleaf dropped to the ground.

"Quit it!" he shouted back. "I give up!"

"Put up your hands and walk toward the lights."

He did so. When he was close to the automobile, the sheriff said, "That you, Alcott Greenleaf?"

"Ayuh." He stopped, five feet from the headlights.

"You been burning down them ice houses, ain't you?"

Greenleaf just looked into the headlights levelly.

"Well, I guess we got you before you burned down this one."

Still he said nothing.

"Alcott Greenleaf, I'm arresting you on suspicion of arson and murder," said the sheriff formally.

"I didn't murder nobody."

"Somebody hung your father. Least, he didn't hang himself."

"That so?"

"Ayuh. I seen him."

"He hung himself."

"How so? There wasn't a thing in the room he could have stood on. Not even his wooden leg."

"Ice."

"Hah?"

"Ice. He read one time about a fellow who got stabbed with an icicle, so there wasn't any weapon. That give him the idea. He told me about it once. He jumped off a block of ice."

"Well, I'll be goddamned."

"That so?"

"Get in the car, son. By the way, you going to cause me any trouble? I don't see how I can handcuff you unless I cuff you hand to leg. That might not be too comfy."

"I'll come peaceful."

As they drove away from the great silent building, the sheriff said, "One thing, anyway. At least we saved one ice house."

"Ayuh."

From behind them came an explosion, muffled yet with great soft power, like the crumbling of an age.

"Goddamnit, Greenleaf. Was that Tidewater?"

"I'd guess."

"Goddamnit." The sheriff paused while he pulled the Nash into a driveway. "Well. I guess we might as well go back and watch her burn."

Maine State Prison
(ca. 1947)

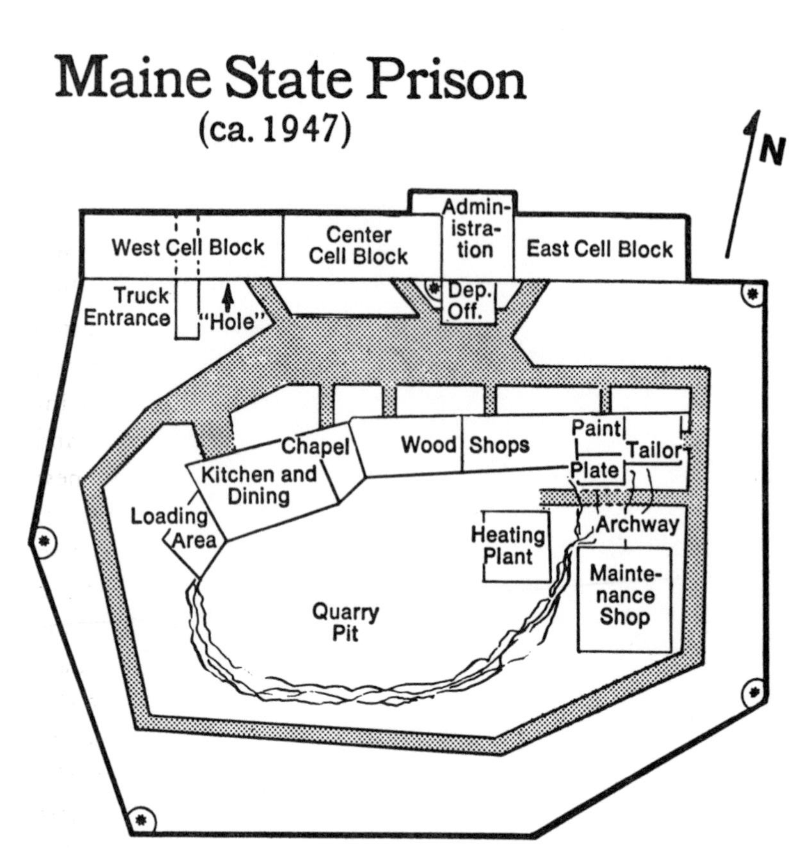

Shaded area = prisoners' walkways

✱ *Guard observation stations*

II Prison

THE long brick-and-limestone prison at Thomaston, snow-covered now this February, emerging from its one hundred twenty-second winter, grimly, sullenly. Statehood, conferred in 1820 upon the populace of Maine by a wrangling nation, brought many new responsibilities, among them that of incarcerating the thieves, smugglers, rapists, murderers, and other malefactors born occasionally to mothers in the new state. Thus a prison—the personal vision of one Dr. Daniel Rose, a six-foot, two-hundred-pound Connecticut physician transplanted to Alna, Boothbay, and finally Wiscasset, a dreamer and a doer both: who chose the site of Limestone Hill in Thomaston in May 1823; who effected its purchase for three thousand dollars from its owner, William King (by happy coincidence his friend and also first governor of the infant state); who designed the acre-and-a-half yard and the rows of narrow, drafty, ill-lit cells; who brought the prisoners north from Charlestown, Massachusetts, confined them at existing institutions, and used them to quarry limestone from the site, forcing them to build their own cells much as a man at gunpoint may be forced to dig his own grave; who brought construction to a conclusion and opened the prison on June 1, 1824, at a total cost to the taxpayers of $30,760.46; and who, without even a sigh of relief, settled at once into the positions of warden and supervising physician.

As the prison aged and grew, it discharged its functions

for the most part stolidly, with few moments of either high honor or great shame. During a twenty-one-year period, however, seven men were executed within its walls, sparks extinguished upon the surface of snow. The third and fourth were hanged shortly before noon on June 25, 1875: Lewis Wagner, handsome and eloquent, enormously popular, still maintaining his innocence of the murder of Anethe Christianson on Smutty Nose Island, standing noosed upon the trap; beside him John True Gordon, convicted of the murders of his brother, sister-in-law, nephew, and niece (a crime to which his neighbor, Charles Green, would later confess), blood-covered and barely conscious from a botched attempt to beat the hangman by suicide, supported by deputies, sitting noosed on a soapbox upon the trap; Wagner gazing down, watching him twitch in the warm spring sunshine and speaking: "Poor Gordon, poor Gordon, you are almost gone."

And with the state's final abolition of capital punishment twelve years later, the prison settled into its patterns of sluggish growth. Men came there, stayed, were released, sometimes returned, escaped (more than fifty in this way declined to complete their sentences), lived, and died. Of the twenty-eight wardens since Daniel Rose, one did not survive his tenure but was murdered by an insane inmate. By 1947 the population had increased to nearly half a thousand, and the walls had stretched out to gather in more than three additional acres. From the outside it seemed as colorless as ever, as though when confined within, men became at once saturnine and emotionless, like vague, troublesome machines.

1

GREENLEAF, close-cropped and empty-faced, sat on a stool at one corner of the great black stamper, pulled a lever once and *bang!* the stamper dropped two feet onto the bed. Slowly it rose, spitting as it did so a shining aluminum rectangle onto a stack near his knee. He could barely read it, the raised silver characters shadowed slightly on the surface:

MAINE
303-131
VACATIONLAND

He pulled the lever again and *bang!* the stamper dropped again, rose again, expelling a second 303-131, mate to the first. He turned a crank on the bed and another on the stamper itself. Then he pulled the operating lever and *bang!* again the stamper dropped and rose, and another bright rectangle slid onto the stack:

Five other men were in the plate shop. A guard sat in the corner on a platform overlooking the whole room, reading an issue of *Police Gazette* folded into a clipboard. On the other side of the shop a man was matching and boxing racks of finished plates, blue with cream numerals, back from the paint shop. Everywhere about the shop zipped a short fat man carrying first a broom, then a stack of blanks, now a polishing rag, next an empty crate: all the while looking at no one and humming to himself in a single tone that reminded Greenleaf of a far-distant outboard motor. Also, at his elbow stood the man who had met him at the Deputies' Office and had brought him from there to the plate shop.

"Greenleaf," the man had said as they stepped out of the office. "Fast Jack Kilgore. I show you where you work and how to get around this joint. It ain't too bad, once you get used to it. Some of the jokers here get really attached to it. Hee. Hee." Fast Jack's voice ran smooth and fast, well-oiled, as if it belonged to a used-car salesman.

They stood looking at the long brick building with its several entrances. "These are the shops, Greenleaf. The farthest one down is the tailor shop, then the paint shop. In back of that's the plate shop, and you'll see that soon enough. Next the wood shops. Up them stairs is the chapel. That's where I work. Finally the kitchen and dining room, which you already been to. Let's take a walk around first before we go to work so you can get the geography straight."

They walked past the dining hall and turned toward the back of the plant. "The prison was built by the first prisoners, who had to quarry some of the rocks for it. It's shaped like a doughnut. You can see the pit here is like the hole in it."

"Well, say there," said Greenleaf. The pit dropped to perhaps forty feet deep, the edge about ten feet away from them. He began walking toward it.

"Hold on! Do you see them red lines? Well, all prisoners have to stay inside them. Or one of them sons of bitches—" he waved to a guard in an enclosed station on the wall, who waved back—"will shoot you in the goddamned stomach."

They continued around the pit. "Them two buildings in back are maintenance and heating. Good job, maintenance. You get to go anywhere. Course, your job ain't that bad. Not real tough, regular hours. Hee. Hee.

"Say, did you hear the one about the bartender interviewing the guy for a job? After the guy leaves, this other fellow comes over to the bartender and says, 'Did you give him the job?' The bartender says yes. 'Well, I know him,' says the second guy. 'He's a drunk, he's a thief, and he's a fairy.' So the next day the bartender says to the first guy, 'Look. If I catch you drinking my hootch, I cut your throat, see? And if I catch you stealing my dough, I cut off your hand, see? Now kiss me, and start work.' Hee. Hee. Hee."

Greenleaf looked at Fast Jack, and then held up his handless wrist. "Ayuh. I worked for that bartender, too."

"Hee. Hee. Say, you're a sport. How'd you like to get something down on the fight tonight? I can get you odds on Gus Lesnevich."

"I don't know nothing about boxing. Who's Gus Lesnevich?"

"Only the light heavyweight champ. He's been in the Coast Guard, sapping Kraut subs, I guess, and so this is his first fight in six years. I can get you four-to-one odds on him. He's up tonight against some jigaboo from Philadelphia named Billy Fox. Some guys figure he's going to get creamed, but if you want to know, four to one is great odds. As good as you'd get outside. Why don't you get in?"

"I ain't got no money."

"Don't worry, Greenie, I'll let you go light. You'll come into some sooner or later."

"Ayuh. Okay."

"How much you want to bet?"

"A buck."

"Hee. Spender, ain't you?"

Greenleaf stopped at an archway that connected the maintenance shop to the tailor shop. A long ramp led past the plate shop down into the pit. "What do they do down there?"

"It's the recreation area, now. In the summer on Sundays they play baseball in it. Paint that goddamned wall green and they'd think they're in Fenway Park. Come on," and he walked under the arch and into the shop.

Afterward, with Greenleaf's newly trained hand steady at the stamper, Fast Jack stood by talking. "I tell you, Greenie, if you want any action, see me. I can get you rookus juice, reefers, you name it. If there was dames in this can, I'd be running them too. Doing God's work and all, I can get around. Hee. Hee."

Bang!

"I been here nine years, Greenie. Hit a bank in Portland and shot a guard. Fucking hero he was. He crapped out and they give me life. So I know my way around this joint. Grew up in Chelsea, outside of Boston, and spent some time in Walpole. This ain't nothing compared to Walpole."

Bang!

"I hear you're doing one-to-three for arson. That the case?"

Bang! Greenleaf looked at him briefly and nodded.

"That how you lost your hand?"

He looked at Fast Jack once more, then back down at the machine.

Bang! . . . Bang!

"Watch this," said Fast Jack. "Hey, Willie!" The guard looked up from his *Police Gazette* for a second. The short fat man came over to them slowly, studying the ground, his broom held in front of him like a feeler. "Willie, this is Greenleaf. He's going to work in here with you guys. Shake hands with him, Willie. Greenleaf, this is Willie Cloutier." He pronounced the name "Cloochee."

Willie stuck his hand out without looking up, and Greenleaf shook it.

"Willie here likes to pull out his tea steeper in front of little girls or little boys, I forget which. Which is it, Willie?"

"N-now, J-J-Jack—" The stammer came out breathless and spitty, heavily French, as he looked earnestly at the ground.

Greenleaf turned back to the machine, hitting the lever—*bang!* still watching the two men as the silver plate popped onto the stack:

"Willie, why don't you show us what you're so proud of, eh? Hee. Hee. Them little Buster Browns don't deserve a man like you. No way. Come on." Fast Jack grinned broadly at Greenleaf, who gazed back at him without expression.

Bang!

"G-godd-d-damnit, J-Jack."

"Come on, Willie, show us. Nothing I like better than a little show. Especially with a wang like yours. Must be longer than that broomstick. Hee. Willie the Fucking Frog, eh?"

An inarticulate wail came from Willie's throat; lowering his head, he rammed into Fast Jack's stomach, a round hornless goat driving him against the stamper: Greenleaf, seeing Fast Jack's hand on the black bed pushing back, hit with quick reflex the lever; the stamper fell like a sledge *bang!* and Fast Jack screamed once clear and shrill like a child and held up his hand glistening with sudden blood, three fingers abruptly terminating now at the third knuckle. The guard jumped up, open-mouthed. The silver plate fell onto the stack:

"Damn," said Greenleaf to himself, "I forgot to change the number."

2

BEFORE dinner the prisoners lined up according to cell blocks in front of the Deputies' Office. One of the deputy wardens called roll and a guard answered for each row: "West Block, Tier Two, present and accounted for, sir!" Just like the Army, thought Greenleaf, when he first heard it; and he stood rigid and erect in the crisp February afternoon, half expecting a master sergeant to come stalking down the columns, slapping protruding stomachs or chucking unbraced chins. But there was none, and the men shuffled silently into the dining hall with their heads low to their tasteless and overcooked food. Just like the Army, he thought again, except that no one could speak to complain about having to eat it.

At 3:25 P.M. the prisoners were marched from the dining hall by twos to their cell blocks. Greenleaf, seventh in a line of twenty-six men, proceeded down a row of cells and stopped facing the seventh from the end. A guard outside the cell row pulled a massive lever, the bars slid open, the prisoners took two steps forward, and the bars slid closed—a short silent contradance, as men's wills bowed to barred doors. He stood like all the others with one hand on the bars while the guard made a sight count. Then he turned and leaned back on them.

He gazed around his cell with curiosity. He had been in it this morning briefly for the first time but now could inspect it at leisure. It was seven feet wide by nine deep, furnished with a bunk, a crapper, a basin and mirror, and a small table and chair. After his week in a bare quarantine cell, he felt some measure of relief to be here, to be part of a community and a routine. Lying back on his bunk, he closed his eyes.

After a bit he heard a faint scratching on the wall at the front of the cell. He went to the end of his bunk and squatted, his back against the bars.

"Ayuh?"

The whisper came to him, barely audible: "You Greenleaf?"

"Ayuh."

"Forker."

"Hah?"

"Forker. My name. What happened to Kilgore?"

"Got his fingers caught in the plate stamper."

"You do it?"

"Accident."

"Any trouble?"

"Nah."

"You best watch. Kilgore's a pisser."

"That so?"

"A real pisser."

"Well, he'll be holding on with his left hand tonight."

"Hah. You down on the fight?"

"Fight?"

"Lesnevich–Fox."

"Ayuh. With Kilgore."

"Who you got?"

"Les-whatever-the-hell-his-name-is. At four to one."

"Sure. Hey. Time for 'Stella Dallas.' "

"What's that?"

"Soap opera on the radio."

"You got a radio?"

"Everybody does. Earphones over your bunk. See you."

He noticed for the first time a pair of earphones and two switches on the cell wall. Putting the phones in his ears, he turned "On/Off–Volume" and heard immediately "—give

Mary the mysterious package? Join us Monday for another episode of 'Mary Noble, Backstage Wife.' "

After a bass voice suggested he use Ajax, the Foaming Cleanser, a rich baritone announced, "We give you now—'Stella Dallas'—a continuation on the air of the true-to-life story of mother love and sacrifice."

He listened without pause to "Stella Dallas," "Lorenzo Jones," "Young Widder Brown," "Just Plain Bill," and "Front Page Farrell." Thus was he brought to the news. He learned first that the day was Friday, February 28, which surprised him vaguely, for he had forgotten already that time would continue to pass even within these walls. He learned that a Senate committee had refused to endorse President Truman's appointment of Gordon R. Clapp as director of the Tennessee Valley Authority; that Senator Capehart from Indiana was prepared to summon John L. Lewis to testify about a pending miners' strike before the Senate Commerce Committee; that the Catholic Youth Organization apparently considered Leo Durocher's marriage to divorced actress Laraine Day the last straw and had withdrawn its support from the Dodgers' Knothole Club; and that Don Frohner, a sixteen-year-old youth from Youngstown, Ohio, had received the death penalty for the murder of a fifty-two-year-old salesman.

He listened with pleasure to the Pepsi-Cola jingle:

> Pepsi-Cola hits the spot,
> Twelve full ounces, that's a lot,
> Twice as much for a nickel too,
> Pepsi-Cola is the drink for you!
> Nickel, nickel, nickel, nickel,
> Trickle, trickle, trickle, trickle,
> Nickel, nickel, nickel, nickel!

Then a sportscaster began to speak, first of basketball and afterward of hockey, with nasal urgency. Greenleaf listened intently as he continued: "Now, in boxing—tonight in Madison Square Garden, light heavyweight champion Gus Lesnevich, returning from a wartime hitch in the Coast Guard, will make his first title defense since he won it in 1941. This is billed as a contest of age versus youth, since the young Billy from Philly is only twenty-three. Fox, with a string of forty-three knockouts against no defeats woven into his gloves, is the heavy favorite to kayo the champ. Odds for the fight have been set at thirty to one."

He removed the headset and went to the front of the cell, where he sat on the floor. Taking off his belt, he softly scratched the buckle against the corner of the wall.

Soon he heard the whisper. "Yeah?"

"Hey. Forker. Remember Kilgore's hand?"

"Yeah?"

"No accident."

"Hah?"

"No accident. I hit him on purpose."

"No shit."

"Ayuh. See you."

He listened to the radio until ten, when Jimmy Durante said good night to Mrs. Callabash, wherever she was—whoever she was. Then he went to sleep. When he awoke at six thirty, he recalled that this was the first day of March and sat up in bed: "Rabbit-rabbit." He turned on the radio, just in time to hear that last night in Madison Square Garden Gus Lesnevich had knocked out Billy Fox in the tenth round.

3

On Sundays the prisoners were allowed to sleep late. The first Sunday of his term he turned on his radio back in his cell after breakfast to discover that it was 8:35 and realized suddenly that he had been awarded an extra half-hour of rest, doubtless at the suggestion of the Lord. He felt grateful. So when the loudspeaker called, "Protestant chapel," an hour later, and all the cell doors slid open simultaneously with electric precision, he stepped with other churchgoers into the cell corridor. Together they marched like Christian soldiers into the crisp bright morning.

The chapel was a large room adjacent to the dining hall and above part of the wood shop, with pews and rails and pulpit sawed, planed, shaped, joined, smoothed, sanded, stained, varnished, waxed, and polished by the unholy hands of convicted felons (who may have performed these labors not to propitiate their sins before God, nor even to demonstrate their contrition before their keepers, but primarily to break the infernal monotony of prison routine. Besides, unlike license plates, road signs, state pamphlets, and the furniture that they built and upholstered, the fruits of this labor would be theirs alone. In this they resembled the original prisoners who built their own prison, except that they did not perceive the analogy and so were spared the humiliation the originals must have felt.).

Greenleaf, simple parishioner, sat in the midst of the congregation. He looked up at the huge bare cross on the wall and the four men who sat on a bench beneath it. Two had on the thin-striped shirt all inmates wore, one was wrapped in black robes, and the other wore a plain dark suit. One of the prisoners held a heavily bandaged hand on his lap; Greenleaf recognized the pale, grim face of Fast Jack Kilgore.

The chaplain, he in black robes, stood up. "Men, I ask you to join me in Hymn 290, 'The Old Rugged Cross.' " The prisoners rose, scuffled, and at his signal began singing: toneless, hopeless, terrible. Five stanzas later they sat down.

"Men," said the chaplain, "we are fortunate to have a

guest preacher here with us today. I want to introduce Reverend Gerald Sweet from Ithaca, New York. Reverend Sweet's sermon this morning is entitled 'Sin, Hell, and Salvation.' "

The man in the suit stood and moved to the pulpit. He carried no papers—a tall man with large hands and a small mouth, graying curly hair, and a face which was mottled and pocked. When he spoke he wagged his head from side to side, and his clear, low voice washed over the prisoners, rising and falling like the tide:

"My brothers, I want to talk to you today first about sin. Most of you probably feel like experts on that subject, I know. In fact, you are probably saying to yourselves right now, 'Why should he tell *us* about sin? We practically invented sin, and that's why we're here in the hole.' But you're wrong there, my brothers, dead wrong. In the Book, Saint Paul wrote, 'For all have sinned and come short of the glory of God.' *All* have sinned. Let's think about that.

"The crimes that brought you here to the hole—theft, fraud, murder, and so on—are real sins, of course, and neither God nor man will argue long that they're not. But there are other sins every person on earth commits every day of his life, sins that may not get him arrested and locked up, but sins that in the end will condemn his soul to hell for eternity. Sins like envy, lust, greed, anger, gluttony. How many of you saw men on the outside, 'successful businessmen' they call themselves, who got to where they were by cheating and robbing poor people blind? How many of you grew up surrounded by people coming home drunk, beating you for no reason? Can anyone here think of someone who has *never* sinned?"

At this point the prisoners began nodding among themselves, wheat before the wind. "Everybody has sinned, brothers. Everybody! And what is sin, exactly? I'll tell you what:

it's cutting yourself away from God. Remember Eve, who ate the apple? Her real sin wasn't apple stealing, it was going against God's word. God told her not to eat the apple, and she ate it anyway. It says in the Book, 'He that doubteth is damned: whatsoever is not of faith is sin.' Eve doubted and was damned. And sometime or other everybody else doubts God's word too; and when they do, they sin.

"So every time you get angry, my brothers, or envious, or lustful, or greedy, you're cutting yourself off from God and condemning your eternal soul to everlasting damnation: 'The soul that sinneth, it shall die.'

"What does hell mean? You should know better than anyone else—you're in it." As he paused, the prisoners started buzzing like startled insects. "Just as your crimes got you thrown into this hole, why that's how the sins of all men get them thrown into the hole of hell. And what is hell, exactly? You know, my brothers, you know. It has always been called the hot place, but it isn't hot at all—it's cold as death, brothers, cold as death. What's the hell of prison when you come right down to it? Not the labor. You don't sweat much here, and the work's not hard. But after work they come and put you in your cell and you're alone and there's the hell of it. After you've done a week or two of solitary, you know what hell is—it's the ice-cold numbness of a man's spirit when he realizes that he's all alone and there isn't anybody who's going to raise a hand to help him.

"Now you are thinking, there's got to be a way out. And there is. Saint Paul wrote to Timothy: 'This is a faithful saying, and worthy of all acceptation that Christ Jesus came into the world to save sinners.' Here is the answer, brothers, the way out: Jesus Christ. He says to us, come. Only repent of your sins and I will take them upon myself. Believe in me and I will carry your soul away from the threat of hell, I will save you from that eternal loneliness and cold. And he was crucified saying this, my brothers, nailed to a cross through his hands and feet with the blood pouring from his side and for nine hours he hung there—not dead, but dying—trying to take our sins upon himself— Ah! the pain—"

He stopped. The prisoners could all see that tears had filled his eyes and were running freely across his face. He raised one hand and then began speaking again, his voice slightly harsh but still controlled, still holding them suspended before him. "Wait, my brothers. Wait. I have one more thing to say. Three years ago I was released from Attica. I was given two-to-five in 1940 for armed robbery. So I know. I know what sin is because I've been there. I know what hell is because I've been there. And I know what salvation is because Jesus has shown me. Like He said, 'I am the way and the truth and the light: no man cometh to the Father but by me.' He saved me, my brothers; let Him save you."

He stood erect in the pulpit, his face streaked with tears like a flag in the rain.

At the end of the service, while the prisoners prayed, the chaplain and Reverend Sweet walked to the back and stood by the door. Then Fast Jack and the other prisoner began to move up the center aisle. As they came to each row of pews, the men there rose and filed out. When it came his turn, Greenleaf stepped into the middle of the aisle between the two ushers and spoke softly, the others passing him by.

"How's the hand?"

"Goddamnit," hissed Fast Jack, "you listen to me—"

"You can forget it, Jack."

"Forget it? By Jesus—"

"I said forget it. I don't want your money anyhow."

"What the hell are you talking about, boy?"

"You owe me four dollars on that fight. I'm telling you to forget it."

He walked up the aisle without looking back, shook Reverend Sweet's hand, and reported to the Deputies' Office. There, the guard on duty checked a list and looked up at him. "You got a visitor, Greenleaf. Mr. Wilcox will take you up."

"Yes, sir."

Another guard led him up iron steps worn shiny to a barred door that buzzed at them. The guard pulled it open, and they marched through to face another door, also barred. As soon as the first closed behind them, the second buzzed open. They entered an empty corral of interviewing booths, interfacing carrels separated by wire mesh. His guide waved to another guard sitting outside the visiting room in a booth like a ticket taker. From a bench against the wall rose a large man in khaki—ponderous whale!—and approached the wall of booths, faintly smiling. It was Sheriff Bartholomew Ware.

"Well, Alcott, what do you know?"

"Well. Goddamn. Not much." Greenleaf smiled back at him. "Good to see you."

"Ayuh. I see they haven't put any fat on you. I seen more meat on a snowflake."

"Nope. I ain't been here that long, though. The food here ain't too bad. It's like the Army."

"That's a shame, then. I was in the neighborhood and thought I'd stop by to see how things are going. I know a couple of these guards. One of them tells me that you already got into a little scrap. Some fellow's hand?"

"Oh, that ain't nothing, Sheriff. Just an accident. Wasn't my fault."

"Ayuh. Well, you be careful."

"You bet."

"Anything you need?"

"Maybe. Do you listen to 'Stella Dallas'?"

"What? The soap opera?"

"Ayuh."

"Nope. But my wife does. Why?"

"I just started listening to it on Friday. Never bothered with the radio before, but now I guess I won't have to miss it too often. I can't figure how her daughter Laurel ever got into that fix with that salesman in the first place."

"I'll have Emmy send you a scorecard. She listens to all of them. Any others?"

"Well, if she listens to 'Just Plain Bill,' she could tell me why she bothers. He ought to have his nose cut off with his razor."

"Okay. Say, did you ever hear 'One Man's Family'?"

"Nope."

"Sunday afternoons. I wouldn't miss it for Thanksgiving dinner. Try it."

Greenleaf nodded and was silent. Finally the sheriff cleared his throat. "Tell me, Alcott. How come are you here?"

"How come? You should know—you put me in."

"I caught you. But you could have got out of coming. Why, any lawyer worth his salt could have pled you temporarily insane because of your father's suicide. You could have gotten off scot-free."

"Maybe so. But even while I was burning those ice shacks, I knew I wouldn't ever be shut of him until I did my time in this place. So when they asked me, I pled myself guilty."

"What's that?"

"The morning of the day Eustis jumped off that ice cake, we had a buster of a fight. I walked out. He told me I was making a mistake, and I told him that I'd make my own mistakes, since he'd already made plenty all by himself. Then he started whining about being crippled and alone without me. Him a cripple? Look what he done to me." He held up his stump angrily, then continued, "I told him to take his wooden leg and shove it up his ass."

Greenleaf's eyes glittered in rage; the sheriff's glazed in shock. "Rough talk, Alcott."

"Ayuh."

"What was he so wrung out about?"

"Hah? Oh. He didn't want me to get married."

"You getting married? I hadn't heard."

"Ayuh."

"Local girl?"

"No. She's from Bath. The old baster hadn't even met her but he was solid against her. We'll do it as soon as I get out."

"I'm glad to hear it."

There was a pause.

"Sheriff, wonder if I could ask a favor."

"Sure thing."

"After I get out, at the wedding? I'd like you to be the best man."

4

SOUTH from St. Georges l'Oueste, Canada, in 1879 came Emile Cloutier to Lewiston, where a sister and brother-in-law had come before and now waited. Short, volatile, handsome in a way, he immediately found work at the Sabbattus Textile Company's factory and shortly afterward found a wife as well, a small, large-eyed woman who proceeded to bear him a child a year for the next sixteen. Twelve lived, of whom the last was a son (the third) named Hilaire Dominic. Babied unmercifully for a time by doting sisters, eventually despised by his mercurial father, Willie Cloutier grew at last into a reclusive butterball, sad, shy, stupid. On April 6, 1917, he celebrated his twenty-first birthday, moving officially into adulthood at the same instant his country moved officially into war.

Neither change particularly bothered him. He would never vote, and he had been working at the same shoe factory since he was twelve, so his majority conferred no new responsibilities upon him. Isolated in illiteracy and indifference, he saw the war as merely a vague, remote event, as irrelevant to his life as the last glacier. However, seven months later this placidity was interrupted when, having registered at the recently created Selective Service Board, Hilaire Dominic Cloutier was drafted by the United States Army.

His parents saw him off at the train station, watched him standing rigid and mute on the platform swirling with boisterous inductees all bound for Fort Devens. "Au 'voir, Hilaire," his mother said. "Reviens." Then she began to cry.

Willie nodded soberly to both of them and, turning away, walked to the train. He looked back at them from the door. His father could see the round face suddenly flood: tears, mucus, and drool springing at once from every facial orifice, the features eroding, dissolving under the rush of waters. Then he disappeared inside the car.

His father shook his head. "Maudzie fou," he said. "Damn fool." Throwing an arm over the shoulders of his still-sobbing wife, he led her home through the gray streets of the city.

Three weeks later Willie returned. He would tell his parents nothing. For a week he would face their raging interrogations like a prisoner of war before a tribunal, refusing to say a word, until at last his father would stalk off in disgust—"Calvaille!"—and his mother would start weeping into her hands. Finally the Cloutiers let out that Willie had received a medical discharge, and he went back to the factory.

For a time life went smoothly. He lived at home, every week giving his paycheck to his mother, every Sunday going to Mass. She soon became proud of him, going as far as bragging of his solid behavior to the neighbors; and even his father grew more relaxed as the steady stream of checks for $17.19 kept flowing into the house.

On weekends he often stood on the fringes of gatherings of old men to listen while they debated and expounded theories of economics, military science, Franco-American culture, labor relations, and any other topic that presented itself. He murmured echoing noises of disgust when they censured the nation's decision to go on Daylight Savings Time. He nodded as they gleefully discussed the appointment of General Foch—a Frenchman!—as the supreme commander of the Allied Forces. He even contributed once when one *vieillard* whirled upon him, saying, "Vous, eh? Aimez-vous cette Prohibition?"

"Non, non," he stammered, meaning that he did not want to be asked (for, since he never drank, he thought nothing of Prohibition one way or the other), but the old man smiled at him, "Eh bien, d'accord," and turning to the others, "Un bon fils, eh?"

As 1918 slid into summer, Willie began to take Saturday walks—not distant, although sometimes ranging a mile or so outside town. Once in a while he brought back souvenirs: a rusty knife, the wing of a dead hawk, stones sparkling with mica, one time a silver dollar, though he found that in a gutter three blocks from his house. Then on July 6, while walking along the Androscoggin River, he saw eight boys between the ages of ten and fourteen swimming naked. He stopped to watch them and, when they came out of the water, approached them with his fly unbuttoned, gracefully displaying a penis no bigger than the body of a dead hummingbird.

The boys ran from him, of course, shrieking with frightened laughter as they scattered into the woods like deer. Willie stood watching them go, then turned and walked back to town, all the while crying softly to himself and swearing "Maudzie Calvaille! Maudzie Christ!" He went directly to Saint Dominic's Church, where in the quiet shadow of the confessional, he told an elderly priest what he had done.

"Mon fils," said the priest, "you have committed a grave sin. I do not understand why you have done this, but I assure you that it is inspired by the devil. Take guard, mon fils, for he leads you to commit this sin in order to drag you into the pits of hell, and condemn your soul to everlasting damnation.

"I am sure that you do not wish to repeat this sin. Therefore I beg you to call upon the Holy Virgin and pray that she help you overcome your sinfulness and be spared the pits of hell. You wish to be saved, n'est-ce pas?"

"Oui, mon père."

But when he arrived home, his parents and a Lewiston policeman were waiting for him. Two of the boys had recognized him and had gone to their fathers, not knowing whether to jeer or to cry. The fathers reacted in horror, as did both the authorities and the Cloutiers senior when they learned of Willie's act. His father passionately disowned him, his mother wept for him one more time, and the policeman led him away. On September 8, 1918, he was sentenced to a term of from four to eight years in the Maine State Prison for "lewd and lascivious behavior," a sentence that he himself believed completely justified—for had he not confessed to both God and man what he had done, and did not both agree that incarceration was the proper penalty for it?

Of the next twenty-nine years Willie spent more than twenty-six in Thomaston. His crimes were always the same—gentle exhibitions—and his sentences were always pronounced without rancor, accepted with gratitude. Within the prison walls he did his work well. Although he had no intimates, he was seldom molested, and most of the inmates tolerated him affectionately. So, when Fast Jack Kilgore had baited him in front of Greenleaf, Willie's response stemmed from surprised distress. Afterward in the shop he spoke to Greenleaf. "You know, that Jack, he is pretty tough. I wish you have not cut off his fingers."

"He'll live."

"Yeah, I know. But he might make trouble."

Greenleaf shrugged, held up his stumped wrist. "We'll just cut a little more off him, then."

Willie's eyes widened. "Maudzie," he muttered and hurried away with his broom. When several weeks passed without repercussions, however, he finally stopped worrying.

From noon until three on Good Friday, Catholic inmates who so wished could attend a service in the chapel, to hear and dream silently upon the seven last words of their Savior. Easter fell late this year—in fact, on April 6, Willie's birthday—so when he left the plate shop at five minutes of twelve on the fourth, he walked in sunshine on warm walkways, smiling, a joyous servant of the Lord.

There were no more than twenty other worshipers present when he arrived. He genuflected beside a rear pew, made the sign of the cross, entered the pew, and knelt, his lips moving. When the priest entered silently, Willie and the others rose. The rhythms of the service—orchestrated standings and kneelings, prayers, responses—swept him up like flotsam, and he bobbed mindlessly in the ebb and flow of the priest's thin voice reading Saint John's account of the Passion: "After this Jesus, knowing that all things were now accomplished, that the Scripture might be fulfilled, said, I thirst. Now there was standing a vessel full of common wine; and having put a sponge soaked with the wine on a stalk of hyssop, they put it to his mouth. Therefore when Jesus had taken the wine, he said, It is consummated! And bowing his head, he gave up the spirit."

Gradually, while the priest read, Willie became aware of a newcomer to his pew. Surreptitiously looking to his left, with a shock he recognized Fast Jack Kilgore, whom he had neither seen nor spoken to since that day in the plate shop. Fast Jack held his hand up to show him the three shortened fingers, healed over now and smooth except for the small twisting scars at the end of the stumps, and smiled. Willie folded his hands together and bent his head. Fast Jack moved closer to him and thrust the hand into the path of his down-turned gaze. In it was a long, shining knife.

"Go to the can, Willie."

Willie closed his eyes.

"Go to the can. And if you say a word, anything, I'll cut you into suet."

Slowly Willie got up and moved into the aisle, Fast Jack right beside him. They walked to the rear of the chapel, where Fast Jack spoke to a guard.

"This man isn't feeling well, sir. I'm taking him to the can."

The guard looked at Willie, who was trembling and sweating. "All right, Kilgore."

As they left, the priest was saying, "One of the soldiers

opened his side with a lance and immediately there came out blood and water." Willie could scarcely hear the words for the beating of his heart.

And in a toilet stall the rape itself: Willie, head held above a hopper, braced by fat forearms, round buttocks trembling, the bride in this strange play; Fast Jack the groom, standing behind and now parting the soft quivering flesh, thrusting deep within it; the two men conjoined as one, moaning, panting, neither aware of pleasure or pain, but rather of consuming rage and hatred and frustration and fear; the sudden expense of fire and immediate cleaving in two once again—one turning in disgust and walking out the door, the other crying quietly and vomiting into the hopper.

When he could stand once more, Willie walked—out of the toilet, past the chapel doors, out the outside landing, and down the rusted iron steps; his face by now expressionless, his eyes glazed over and empty, only his mouth moving slightly; stepping slowly but deliberately into the sunshine, turning west past the west cell block on his right and the dining hall and loading area on his left, keeping within the red lines of the walkway as it swung south

(while in the plate shop Greenleaf sat at his stamper, creating stop signs out of metal and oblivion; and while within the chapel Fast Jack leaned back against a pew and trembled, the others prayed, and the priest spoke of miracles and sacrifice, of death and coming resurrection, of sin and forgiveness, of atonement and eventual salvation);

his steps still steady as he continued around the walkway to the south side of the yard, soft white clouds scudding across the April sky, three guards watching him from their stations on the wall—and then he stopped.

The guard in the southwest station, closest to him, called through his loudspeaker: "Move on, prisoner!"

Willie stood immobile, rigid, insentient. Then he broke for the edge of the quarry pit and leaped out, sinking from the gazes of the three guards, who could not see clear to the bottom. He turned in the air as he fell, landing at last on the back of his neck, bounced once, and lay still.

5

WHEN the reveille bell rang at 7:45 on Easter Sunday, it was raining, and Greenleaf was already awake. Slowly, deliberately, he swung his legs out of his bunk onto the floor. He put on his clothes with the same grim care. Then he sat back on the edge of his bunk, methodically punching his forearm with his fist.

At breakfast he sat next to Forker, his neighbor, the two of them spooning gluey oatmeal into their mouths. Forker bent to his bowl and whispered without moving his lips, "You up to something, Greenleaf?"

He shook his head.

"Good. Don't want to get carried away."

Greenleaf turned to stare at him eye for eye. Forker looked down hastily and said nothing more.

At 9:35 Protestant prisoners marched through the rain to the chapel for their celebration of the nineteen-hundred-year-old miracle of resurrection, Greenleaf among them. When the others stood, he stood also, and he sat when they sat; but he neither heard nor spoke a word during the service, only watched—intently, furiously—the relaxed worshipful figure of Fast Jack Kilgore.

At the end the prisoners (excepting Greenleaf) sang "Jesus Christ Is Risen Today." As the final Alleluia echoed hoarsely against the ceiling, Fast Jack and the other usher started to move up the aisle, releasing successive pews. Greenleaf stood stony until they came abreast of his row; as awkward as a mechanical soldier he shuffled toward them. When he reached the end of the pew, his eyes lifted in surprise. "Why, Fast Jack, as I breathe."

He suddenly lowered his right shoulder and drove his fist deep into the other man's stomach, who buckled and fell backward, bringing up his knees to his chest in pain and reflex, simultaneously fumbling at his sleeve. In his hand a knife flashed; Greenleaf dived at him, catching the blade on his handless forearm, and struck again with the fist in the face this time, feeling the nose give way beneath it. Blood gushed, the knife clattered away, and then the guards were upon them.

They were taken to an interrogation room with the two guards and one of the deputy wardens.

"Bastard," said Fast Jack, a towel over his nose. "He went for me. He even pulled that knife on me."

"Bullshit," said Greenleaf. He held up his bandaged arm. "If I'd had that knife, I wouldn't have got cut up. And he would have."

The deputy warden said, "Shut up, both of you. Kilgore, it seems to me that you've been setting a pretty pisspoor example lately to be working in the chapel. First that problem with your hand, and now here you are mixed up in a fight. Tomorrow why don't you report back to the wood shop."

Fast Jack's voice trembled in fury. "Yes, sir."

"And you, Greenleaf. I think you'd better get some time by yourself to cool off and think about the inadvisability of assaulting someone with or without a deadly weapon. Two weeks in the hole and loss of all accumulated good time."

"Yes, sir."

He was escorted through corridors and down flights of stairs to the basement of the west cell block, where he and his conductor were met by a wide-shouldered guard with short brown hair. "Christmas, Peter, who's this guy, eh? Trouble?"

"Not much, Frank. He's Greenleaf. Greenleaf, meet Mr. Fortin. This young buck got into a scrap with another prisoner, that's all, and he'll be visiting with you for two weeks."

"Yah? You ever been up here before, Greenleaf?"

"Nope."

"Well, I tell you, boy. I ain't too hard to get along with. I put you in the cooler block to start with. If you don't give me no trouble, I don't give you none either. If you do—Christmas. Come here." He led them to a corridor lined with six heavy blank doors. With a large key he opened one of them and snapped a light switch. Inside was a barred wall and beyond it a cell: painted dull red, windowless, completely bare save for a small hole in one corner of the floor. "That's a hole cell. Two weeks in there is no fun, you bet."

Greenleaf nodded.

Fortin conducted him to a small row of cells, opened one, and ushered him inside. "If you need anything, don't yell. I make a tour every hour."

"Yes, sir."

"You eat at eight, eleven, and four. Bread and milk." He closed the door. The cell was furnished with a plank bunk, a mirror and basin, and a hopper. He sat on the bunk and gazed through the bars to four small basement windows high on the wall beyond. Through these he could see that the clouds had broken and the sun was now shining.

6

On Sunday morning, April 20, the guard Fortin came cheerily to Greenleaf's cell. "Well, you're out now, boy, and I hope to Christmas this is the last I see of you."

"Yes, sir."

"It's a beautiful morning out there. Going to chapel today?"

"I guess not."

"Ah, now, you should, eh? To thank the good Lord you're out? You don't have to worry about your buddy Kilgore no more, anyhow."

"Ayuh, I know. He got hooked out of that chapel job when I come up here."

"Yah, but I guess nobody told you. Last Friday he had an accident in the wood shop. Hurt bad, I hear. They had to take him up to Bangor to the hospital. He still ain't back."

"What happened to him?"

"Christmas, I don't know. I just heard he got cut up by a saw. Come on, let's go, you can make it to breakfast now."

He went, whistling softly and tunelessly to himself. Outside, the air was warm and moist. Birds twittered faintly from the trees beyond the walls, and by the walkway a sparrow pecked intently at an invisible seed in the grass. In the dining hall once more he ate his first bowlful of oatmeal in two weeks and listened to Forker's whisper:

"How was the hole?"

"Not too bad. Bad enough."

"How'd you like Fortin?"

"Hah. All right to me. But he beat hell out of one joker. Who called him a dumb frog."

"Jesus."

"Ayuh. You been there?"

"About everybody has. Sooner or later."

"What happened to Kilgore?"

"Got hurt."

"Ayuh. How?"

"Later."

He looked up to see a guard cruising near them. He grinned, then plugged his ebullience inside himself with a mouthful of oatmeal.

Back in their cells Forker told him that a number of prisoners had reacted unhappily to Willie Cloutier's suicide when the whole story began circulating; that Greenleaf's assault upon Fast Jack Kilgore had further focused their sense of outrage; that finally on Friday an informal committee of four men had confronted Fast Jack in the wood shop, demanding he either expiate his guilt for Willie's death himself or accept their penalty for it ("Christ, they were going to kill him," said Forker); that Fast Jack, reading the deal accurately, wheeled about, withdrew his penis from his pants, held it against the edge of a bandsaw, and—as the four judges scattered from his vicinity—hit the switch, the glans falling from the shaft like the severed head of a snake.

Greenleaf felt strong gratitude for the mysterious but effective methods of the Lord and so, when the call echoed in the cell block, decided to attend chapel services for the third (and incidentally the last) time during the period of his confinement. There the chaplain somberly described the wages of sin to his congregation, who listened dispassionately, perhaps condescendingly. "Many of you men may be aware of the expression 'an eye for an eye.' It comes from the twenty-first chapter of Exodus, where God, having given Moses the Ten Commandments, explains what the consequences of breaking these laws should be. The extremity of the law, says God, demands 'life for life, eye for eye, tooth for tooth, hand for hand, foot for foot, burning for burning, wound for wound, stripe for stripe.' "

"Prick for prick, too," whispered Forker beside him.

Suddenly sputtering, snorting, tears streaming from his eyes, Greenleaf rose and pushed blindly for the aisle; he pushed past the astonished guard and into the corridor; outside the doors he leaned against the wall when he saw Forker also emerging and gasped, "Cock for cock"; whooping with laughter, arm in arm, the two men stumbled out from under the grace of God into the warm sun.

III Marriage

THE august splendor of ritual and pomp, some of its origins rooted by now so deeply in the primeval earth that they may have been forever obscured, flashes with brilliance through the chill gray mists of Westminster Abbey on this Thursday, of London in November, of England and the world in 1947. It is a royal wedding, an event of great hope and joy and promise for the future, commemorated both by national holiday and by public spectacle, but finally by the inevitable album of photographs: the procession through Trafalgar Square, portraits of the principals, the vast crowds outside the palace gates, and the ceremony itself.

In the foreground stand the two small kilted princes, William of Gloucester and Michael of Kent, holding the fifteen-foot train with stubborn truculence as if they were about to fold a bedsheet; four steps above them the four figures like dolls set in a row, from the right best man and groom and bride and father—the Marquess of Milford Haven, Lieutenant Philip Mountbatten, Princess Elizabeth Alexandra Mary, and King George VI of England—the two naval officers ramrod straight, the princess an erect white cone in her spreading gown and veils, and the king slightly turned toward his daughter, thus appearing perhaps just that much frailer than his regal daughter and his imminent son-in-law; and above them the robed and mitered bishops and archbishops, one of whom has already stepped forward and with care and awe and love is beginning to read:

"Dearly beloved, we are gathered together here in the sight of God and in the face of this congregation, to join together this Man and this Woman in holy Matrimony; which is an honourable estate, instituted of God in the time of Man's innocency, signifying unto us the mystical union that is between Christ and his Church; which holy estate Christ adorned and beautified with his presence, and first miracle that he wrought in Cana of Galilee; and is commended of Saint Paul to be honourable among all men: and therefore is not by any to be enterprized, nor taken in hand lightly, or wantonly, to satisfy men's carnal lusts and appetites, like brute beasts that have no understanding; but reverently, discretely, advisedly, soberly, & in the fear of God; duly considering the causes for which Matrimony was ordained.

"First, It was ordained for the procreation of children to be brought up in the fear and nurture of the Lord, and to the praise of his holy Name.

"Secondly, It was ordained as a remedy against sin, & to avoid fornication, that such persons as have not the gift of continency might marry, and keep themselves members of Christ's body.

"Thirdly, It was ordained for the mutual society, help, and comfort, that the one ought to have of the other, both in prosperity & adversity. Into which holy estate these two persons present come now to be joined. Therefore if any man can shew just cause, why they might not lawfully be joined together, let him now speak, or else hereafter for ever hold his peace."

And after this and the rest of it, the plightings of troth, the blessings, the trumpetings and cheerings, are finished and done; after too the miters and chasubles, the stoles and cinctures, the maniples and pallia and pectoral crosses are folded and laid aside and put away; and finally after the children and guests and the crowds, not to mention the royal couple, are in bed and sleeping or not sleeping: the Abbey lies in darkness, still reverberating faintly with echoes of affirmation, with intimations of new life.

1

TOGETHER in the Nash (two and a half years older now and looking much more than that) they rode southwest into Lincoln County, entering the town of Waldoboro, the three of them: Sheriff Ware, his wife Emily, and Greenleaf, pale and small in his new blue suit, serge with wide lapels and loose floppy pant legs.

"They give you that suit, Alcott?" asked the sheriff.

"Ayuh."

"Looks pretty snappy."

"They make them there in prison. They give me fifty bucks, too."

"Well, I'll be damned. I thought that was just in the movies."

"Uhuh. They call it gate money."

"Gracious, Alcott," said Emily. "Fifty dollars. My. That was nice of them, wasn't it?"

"Ayuh. Well. Except I guess I earned it."

"I guess you did," said the sheriff. "Comes to less than half a dollar a week."

"There ain't much money in license plates."

"No, I suppose there ain't." He paused. "Say, we got a present for you too. Talking of presents. Give it to him, Emmy."

She handed him a small box in bright paper, which he carefully unwrapped. "Well there. Hah. Just what I need." He smiled at each of them and held up the gift: a shining silver Zippo, brushed chrome.

"I was afraid you'd mind, but Bee said you told him you lost yours and so we guessed you would value another."

"Ayuh. And I figured you had earned the right to carry it."

"Well, thanks."

In silence next they rolled on, the crowned roads wet with the mixed rain and snow following over them like a dirge on this March 11, 1949. Bare brown spots littered the white fields past which they drove. Skeletal trees stood at the roadside, their roots buried in dirty snow, their upper limbs whipping in the weather. Emily spoke:

"Must feel nice to be free."

"Some nice, Mrs. Ware."

"I bet you can't wait to see your girl. Now, let's see. What was her name?"

"Margaret."

"Pretty name. Margaret. Margaret what?"

"Fields."

"Bee tells me you two are getting married. I think that's wonderful, that she would wait for you and now you have someone to come home to."

"Ayuh."

"Well, now. When is the wedding?"

"I don't know. Pretty soon, I guess. I got to talk to Margaret about it."

"Good Lord, Alcott. There ain't no rush. Why you just got out of one penal institution. There ain't no need to turn right around and shut yourself up in another one."

"Now, Bee."

"Just kidding the boy, Emmy. He knows that. Right?"

"You bet, Sheriff."

The sheriff leaned over his wife's knees and turned on the two-way radio. After a minute or so static began to buzz and crackle and snap. He picked up the microphone and shouted into it.

"Sheriff Ware calling base. Sheriff Ware calling base. Come in, please. Ed, you there?"

The static continued. The sheriff shouted louder.

"Ware to base. Ware to base. Come in."

"Goodness, Bee. Why don't you just open the window? They can hear you all the way to Portland."

"Goddamned science. Listen to it. Sounds just like a bowl of Rice Krispies." He shut it off.

Greenleaf stretched and yawned, then settled against the car door. The windshield wipers cut arcs of transparence each across its own pane, rubber razors whispering over the glass. With each stroke his eyelids fell lower until they closed entirely, and he was asleep. His dreams were confused, of prison, involving guards and women who moved together outside the cells that held him and the other prisoners. They screamed as they walked past him but he could not understand what they meant, or even if they were screaming at him. When he woke up to the renewed spluttering of the radio, the Nash was crossing the long bridge over the Sheepscot into Wiscasset, the hulls of the *Luther Little* and her anonymous sister—the two broken and deserted schooners—lying in the river there like a pair of huge discarded public library lions. The sheriff spoke loudly into the microphone. Apparently it had mustered enough range to broadcast from the bridge to the courthouse atop the hill a half-mile ahead of them.

"Ayup. Good, Ed. We'll just shoot up to Whitefield then, and take him home. Ware clear."

Halfway up the Main Street hill they turned right and

drove north along the Ridge Road, past the old county jailhouse where Greenleaf had spent the several months before, during, and after his trial. The Thomaston prison had seemed luxurious by comparison to this: a gray, squat, cold building erected in 1809 out of huge granite blocks, unquestionably secure during those brawling bawdy days of Wiscasset's prime, a century and more earlier (in that era many a sailor had spent some or all of his liberty in that jail); a structure of stone slab ceilings and forty-one-inch-thick walls and cell doors the keys to which weighed three pounds, all of which was sufficient to keep the miscreants entrusted to it as close as cloistered nuns. Now it sat hunched high on the bluff, staring gloomily across the wide gray river, still the silent mother of men's despair.

"Want to stop and visit?" asked the sheriff.

"I guess not." He compressed his mouth, watching the familiar road rush toward him.

"Alcott," said Emily. "Speaking of weddings, do you think Stella Dallas will let her daughter marry that fellow?"

"What?"

"Laurel, on the radio show."

"Oh, that. You know what, Mrs. Ware? I been listening to them radio shows for two years straight. I had it. I ain't ever going to listen to another one again."

"Guess I can't blame you for that."

"Say," said the sheriff, "I hear they convicted Axis Sally yesterday."

"Who's that?"

"A woman radio announcer for the Nazis during the war. She comes from right up in Portland. A local girl, almost. She used to read German propaganda reports in English to the G.I.'s. Like Tokyo Rose did. You were in the Pacific. Did you ever hear Tokyo Rose?"

Greenleaf shook his head.

"Well, they convicted Axis Sally of treason. She'll probably spend a long time in some cell somewhere."

"Hell. They ought to just let her go."

"You think so?"

"Goddamn right. Nobody ought to have to go in the slam. Especially if all they did was broadcast on the radio against the goddamned war. And never if they're a woman."

"Why, Alcott," said Emily. "I think you'll make a dandy husband."

Greenleaf looked out of the window at the wet countryside. They crossed the Alna bridge, and the Nash bumped along the narrow road. He felt his heartbeat quicken. Head Tide, and then he saw the sign, more weatherbeaten than ever after the last two winters, barely legible—SCRAP METALS, USED AUTO PARTS, BOUGHT AND SOLD. E. GREENLEAF & SON—and the blue Pontiac—LOSE LIPS SINK SHIPS! REMEBER PEARL HBR!—and the piles of rusted junk and the gray unpainted house and he was home.

2

THE town of Bath lay twelve miles southwest of Wiscasset in Sagadahoc County. It had been founded in 1660 on the Kennebec River, where deep protected water and sloping shores and accessible stands of timber gave it in time the nickname "Cradle of Ships"; here Jonathan Philbrick and his sons built and launched the area's first schooner in 1743, and here the men following them built and launched hundreds more, among them the *Wyoming,* the largest wooden ship ever sailed; the *Thomas W. Lawson,* the only seven-masted schooner ever built; the *Ranger,* the successful defender of the America's Cup in 1937; J. P. Morgan's fabulous yacht the

Corsair: in all a rich tradition to turn toward the war effort. Indeed, Bath had rejoiced in World War II, and in 1942 the Bath Iron Works launched a new destroyer every twenty-eight days.

Money ran like water through the town then. Women riveted and welded, men worked double shifts, and every Friday the paychecks flooded the streets. A man named Lindall Grote, the owner of a small diner near the shipyard, made a small fortune by borrowing thousands of dollars from the bank each payday and standing at the gate with his cash-box, charging the men ten cents each to cash their checks. Even today Lindall drives a Cadillac, and he was then merely wringing out the wash.

Twenty-two-year-old Margaret Fields and her nine-year-old sister, Evelyn, came from Portland to Bath in 1942, two recent orphans brought by need and opportunity and fate to this boom town. No riveter she, Margaret found work at Lindall Grote's place, "Mary's Diner: The Best Cup of Coffee in Bath." Which was not saying much. There she slung hash and hustled beers and absorbed osmotically what she could from the silver flowing all around her. When the war ended and the gush slowed to a trickle, she stayed on until after a time her identity gently merged with the restaurant. Some of the patrons began calling her Mary (no Mary had ever worked at Mary's; Lindall Grote had named it after his mother-in-law, who shortly afterward—probably from the shock—died); and her sad bumpy face shone with the same sweaty luster as the counters she so religiously and unremittingly polished.

She and her sister lived in a two-room apartment above the diner. Evelyn was a trial to her. She was sent regularly to school but loathed it, watching with hot, hollow eyes the antics of her classmates, suffering them contemptuously, sullenly, bitterly. At nine she was bony and thin, but when she reached eleven the first menstrual blood spotted her sheets, and by thirteen her body teemed overripe and panting beneath the thin cotton dresses with which it was covered.

In 1946 her seventh-grade class was an unruly lot under the direction of a slight, sandy-haired man of twenty-six named Francis Nesbitt. At the outbreak of the war he had been classified 4-F because of an awesome case of hemorrhoids. ("I never seen nothing like it," said the medic who examined him. "That poor bastard had bigger piles than a brickyard.") So he returned to the state university and after his graduation accepted a position in his home town as a teacher at the Henry Wadsworth Longfellow Elementary School for the salary of $1,125 per annum, and was still there four years later, standing helplessly in a high-ceilinged classroom with huge windows and a dusty American flag in front of thirty-eight unwashed and raging children, Canute impotent before the tide.

"Two-bit, Nesbitt, hasn't got a dollar, sat on a tack and should have heard him holler," sang the girls at recess, hopping sparrowlike over their jump ropes.

"Half-wit, Nesbitt, ate shit and had a fit," called the boys after school, darting like flickers across the playground.

Francis heard them all, could scarcely help hearing them, and inarticulate frustration boiled within him. While it worked and grew, however, he began to notice that Evelyn was somehow set apart from the others, was like him a sort of pariah. He seemed to feel some vague kinship with her when he looked out over the sea of small ruffians and picked out that scornful face, believing perhaps that her disdain was directed entirely against her peers and that she was allied with him against them. In this he was mistaken in her motives and worse in his own. It was her blossoming sexuality that had attracted him, not her aloofness; and like a moth with bright fire he began surreptitiously to flutter around her, desperately trying to interest, to enchant her—meanwhile ignoring the reality of his own enchantment. Secretly he played to her alone, totally excluding the others: every fact and joke he uttered, every cipher and word he chalked, every motion, all was for her benefit; and he watched her face narrowly for some response. Here too he was frustrated, for Evelyn paid him no attention whatever, never gave him sign she even heard a word he said.

Her schoolwork had always been a thin trickle, but in Nesbitt's class it dried up altogether. She not only failed tests, she returned them to him blank. She refused to answer questions put to her in class, refused in fact to speak, would only look back at him with that virulent and smoldering stare. And so, on one Friday in the spring term, having somehow convinced himself that he should try to forestall her almost certain failure, Nesbitt spoke to her at the final bell, his high clear voice rising over the clamor of scrambling feet and slamming desks: "Evelyn. Would you stay after school, please."

She made no reply, but only glared back at him and hunched over in her seat. The other children (from whom she expected no compassion and who indeed felt none) rushed out without looking back.

He rose, walked to the door, and shut it. When he was back at his desk, he said, "Come up here and look at this test."

Slowly she approached him, her hands clenched at her sides, her eyes burning at him. He was indicating a blank sheet of paper with one finger, not looking up yet intensely aware of the sounds and smells she created in her passage. He spoke with a slight harshness.

"Just look at this, Evelyn. You didn't write anything on it. Only your name."

Still silent she stood beside him. She arched her back, thrusting her pelvis in front of her like a shield; and as he turned to look at her, she closed her eyes and started to sway her hips gently, birches in a summer breeze.

The teacher caught his breath and then felt something—a stretched wire—snap within him; he snatched at her, panting hoarsely, tiny flecks of foam falling from his mouth, his fingers scrabbling and tearing at the thin cotton and at her legs, buttocks, and pudendum; the dress and worn underpants shredded easily from her body, exposing the dark thick-tufted triangle of pubic hair; he half stood, pushing her undershirt and what remained of her bodice up to her neck. She stepped back deliberately from him, watching him stumble to his knees; and at last she spoke, her voice childish, yet low and vicious: "That's my pussy."

And he could not answer, could only move toward her desperately, all fear and shame and pity and terror purged from him by the purity and simplicity of his lust. She came forward, took hold of his ears like the handles of a wheelbarrow, and pulled his face to her bush.

"Kiss it. Lick it."

Maddened, he seized her haunches in his hands and crushed her into him. He swirled his lips and tongue around the vulva, tasting the electric hair and hot musky juice, like a bear sucking bees and honey both from the hive. He moaned, fine and thin and clear; finally small passion broke inside her, and she released a fiery stream of urine into his mouth and across his face. He fell back coughing.

With the rags of her clothes hanging from her neck, she went to the coatroom, where she took down an old yellow slicker and put it on. At the classroom door she looked back at the man still kneeling on the floor and spoke: "I want a A."

There were no public repercussions for either the teacher or the girl. During the rest of the year he continued in front of the class, more subdued and deliberate than before, perhaps, but with no apparent guilt or shame. Evelyn sat staring at him from her seat, as silent as ever with scorn and heat and contempt hanging over her like mist over water on a cold morning; and in June she brought home and showed to Margaret, shocking her into wondering silence, an absolute and total anomaly that she had never possessed before and never would again—a rank card completely covered with A's.

Characteristically, Margaret neither questioned nor even suspected the validity of the piece of cardboard that bristled like a porcupine with its erect spiny letters, but simply determined its significance and tried to accept it, to expand herself so she could absorb it as if she were some sort of vast phlegmatic sponge. Still, it was a miracle, and the next day she told Lindall Grote about it as she handed him his eleven o'clock cup of coffee, her voice harsh and earnest.

"I tell you, Lin, there wasn't a single thing on it but her name and A's. Spooky. I never see anything like it. Maybe she won't end up taking in laundry after all."

"Hah. Maybe not." Lindall seldom expressed his opinions aloud—for one thing, the practice was bad for business—and what he actually thought about the rank card and what it meant to Evelyn (which thoughts, indeed, were not far removed from the truth) remained unspoken. "What's she going to do for the summer now that school's out?"

Margaret lit a cigarette and tossed the match into a tin ashtray on the counter. She exhaled slowly, speaking with the same wind so the words came out even more hoarsely than usual, the smoke blurring the consonantal stops and spirants, roughening the glides and laterals.

"Says she wants to work. Maybe she'd like a kitchen job."

"Hah. Doubt that."

"You're probably right. You know, I'll be glad when she's old enough to get married. She needs a man to take care of her."

The poor devil that marries that little bitch will feel the fires of hell a bit sooner than he expected, thought Lindall, though he said only, "That might be the ticket. Hah. But how about you, Maggie? Why don't you get a husband for yourself?"

"Huh. Who'd want to marry me?"

From outside a sudden and growing din broke over their conversation: the roar of an unmuffled engine punctuated with backfirings and rattlings and honkings, so that the two of them rushed to the front door in consternation and fear to look up Washington Street, which ran down a steep hill toward them to where it intersected Center Street right in front of the diner, hearing now also the sweet shrill scream of a child. At the door they saw the scene frozen for an instant in tableau: in the intersection at the base of the hill a car, stalled; above it descending a truck, battered and rusted, its body filled beyond belief with scrap metal and a homemade wrecking hoist, not thirty feet from the bottom and not about to stop either; above that, the serene elm-lined street and the houses and the clear blue sky. They watched bug-eyed as the truck swerved onto the sidewalk, snapped a hydrant at the base—leaving a small geyser to mark its fearful wake—and then thundered around the stalled car, across the intersection, and into a telephone pole not seven feet away from them, where it stopped.

The impact of the crash threw both of the truck's doors open. Right before their eyes the driver leaped from the cab—even before the junk in the body had settled—and commenced kicking the left front tire. Margaret noticed that his left arm terminated in a stump at the wrist.

"Goddamn them brakes. Goddamn them to hell." Then he saw them standing in the diner's doorway, both slack-jawed and speechless.

"Do you have a telephone? I guess I had a little accident."

3

LOOKING back afterward, Margaret was never clear in her mind of the chronology of that summer. Certain events stood above the others in her memory, rising like sunflowers from a field of daisies; these she was able to recall in space but not in time. From Greenleaf's noisy arrival at the doorstep of the diner to his departure into history nearly three months later, she drifted over misty seas of bliss.

Others noticed a change working in her before she was conscious of it herself, even before there was reason for it to occur. They remembered, for instance, when she began wearing the ribbons in her hair. Greenleaf had been appearing regularly for an afternoon beer at Mary's—it was then a couple of weeks after his accident there—though he had not yet indicated any unusual interest in Margaret. Yet she (who had never before evidenced any inclination toward personal ornamentation) came downstairs for the lunch shift this day sporting a pair of bows tied of three-inch-wide red satin ribbon, one on each side of her head, looping off two shocks of her coarse hair like the ears of a great squat spaniel tricked out on a Christmas morning.

"Well, Jesus," said Lindall mostly to himself.

"Morning, Lin."

"Ayuh. Sure is. And how are you today, Maggie?"

"Good."

"I bet. You look spectacular with them bows on. Sort of a modern-day Scarlett O'Hara."

"Oh, yes. Nice, ain't they? Evelyn left them on the dresser last night, so I thought I'd try them on."

"Well, they are brighter than bracelets on a butterfly."

She blushed, and though it was only eleven o'clock, Lindall wonderingly drew himself a beer.

During the day most of her customers noticed the bows and commented, either to compliment or fondly to rag her about such extravagant frippery. She only smiled at them, oblivious of any of their teasing. Late in the afternoon Greenleaf came in. He ordered a beer, never taking his eyes off her; and when she returned to set the glass shyly in front of him, he said quietly, "Those look some good." Every day thereafter for the rest of the summer she wore big red bows in her hair, and within a week it was common knowledge in Bath that she and Alcott Greenleaf were going around together.

She herself did nothing to steer the course of their relationship. He did that. Passively and unquestioningly she followed his leads or at the very least found herself being moved in their directions. When he said wait, she waited; go, she went; gee or haw, she geed or hawed. It was not that she had been swept off her feet exactly, but her immense passivity seemed to have been wrenched afloat by a flood tide, sudden and completely unexpected.

Of her sister she saw little during that summer and, awash as she was with thoughts of Greenleaf, she did not at first realize her neglect. Since she got up at five thirty to open the restaurant, their paths during the day crossed only at meals. At night Evelyn was out to all hours; but Margaret seldom noticed because she did not often spend her evenings at home either, but was out riding in one or another of Greenleaf's reclaimed trucks.

One night Evelyn came in to find them embracing on the sofa. "Well, Margaret, ain't you something?" her voice bleak with disgust.

They separated slowly. Margaret smiled vaguely at her.

"Evelyn. Alcott, this here's my sister. This is Mr. Greenleaf, honey."

"Hi there, sissy."

"Don't call me 'sissy.' I ain't your sister."

"In kind of a nasty mood, ain't she, Margaret?"

"Evelyn. You don't need to talk to him like that."

"You going to marry Margaret?"

"She don't waste much time on chitchat, either. Gets right down to what's on her mind."

"Evelyn, what are you doing with that pack of cigarettes? You're too young to be smoking. Anyway, it looks cheap. Put it up."

"You got a light?"

"She looks old enough to me. I'd let her go, Margaret. She ain't going to stop just because you tell her, anyhow."

"Oh, all right, Evelyn. Go ahead. It's your funeral."

"You got a light?"

"You bet, sis." And with a flick of his Zippo he put a flame to the end of her cigarette, staring all the while at Margaret. At the same time he snapped it shut, he winked. Margaret giggled.

For them that summer in Maine passed swiftly and sweetly. Each day the cool Atlantic washed over the rocks of the coast, and the blue northwest wind sent puffy white clouds sailing across the sky. Or when the rains set in for a spell, the leaves of roadside maples and birches were rinsed clean of dust, and grasses everywhere greened and grew thick. Ospreys that had returned to their rough nests to brood brought at last their young into the air with wheelings and soarings and sharp high cries of joy.

Surrounded by such extravagance, Greenleaf and Margaret spent days together walking the crowded beach at Reid State Park or lying side by side in a field overlooking Merrymeeting Bay. At such times, insulated from the rest of the world by her adoration, he grew almost expansive, speaking at length about people he had known and places he had seen while in the Army. But even then he would never talk about his own role in the Pacific.

When he paused during one of these moments, Margaret happened to ask him how he had come to lose his hand. He was slow to answer. "Ayuh," he said finally. "On Guam. It was an accident."

He fell into such a silence that she felt faint and frightened. "Please, Alcott," she said when she could stand it no longer. "I won't ask again. Nothing. None of it matters, anyhow."

"Hah? Oh. That's right. It don't." And by degrees he relaxed and began to talk with her again.

Despite her docility, however, she did refuse him one thing: the premature (viz. premarital) possession of her maidenhead. Every magazine article and movie of her experience had told her that without that precious flower she would be disgraced and left unfit for marriage. So she offered a compromise: the full range of her body above the waist, but nothing below it. For him this was entirely satisfactory. He was shy and, never having had a woman before, would almost certainly have been frightened away had he successfully seduced her; besides, he held the same moral code she did and had no desire to ruin her. On summer evenings, then, they lay together on a blanket in some isolated meadow beneath the stars, nude to their navels, kissing and grappling and moaning.

Most surprising to them both at these moments was Margaret's capacity for passion. Something inside her would give way, and she would grasp his left forearm with frenetic strength, pressing the stump of his wrist against her body and slapping her breasts hard against it, the nipples shining dark purple in moonlight. "Hard, Alcott. Hard," she would rasp; and lost to the particular mystery breaking within her, he would press himself against her body until his own tension itself broke, spilling into his pants. Then they would lie there empty, their recent heat dissipating upward into the cool night.

Friday, August 30, began just like any other day in Margaret's sweet-flowing summer. At five thirty she came stumbling down the stairs into the restaurant, wearing a bright yellow dress and those perpetual red bows, humming hoarsely to herself. She was still humming when Lindall came in at quarter to six, croaking through a tune he could not recognize with certainty, but one he guessed was probably "To Each His Own," which a week before had been named number one on "Your Hit Parade" and of which he knew Margaret was extremely fond. A second later all doubt was removed when, filling a napkin holder, she burst into song, a huge goldfinch with the voice of a grackle: "To each his own, I've found my own, and my own is you."

"Morning, Maggie. You sound happy today."

"Morning, Lin. Sure is pretty."

"Ayup. Sure is."

She resumed humming and, like a massive bumblebee, went about her morning business.

By seven thirty Mary's had become a hubbub of breakfasters—talking, clattering, laughing, clinking, scraping, tramping across the floor, all punctuated by the occasional ring of the cash-register bell. Suddenly Greenleaf appeared in the door, his face rigid with fury. He walked over to where Margaret was setting cups of coffee in front of four men.

"Margaret."

"Why, Alcott. You here for breakfast? That's nice."

"Margaret. Let's get out of here."

"Huh? But I got to serve till ten."

"Goddamnit, Margaret. Come."

Somehow, during this exchange the restaurant had fallen into a profound silence, the men musing over their food, no one looking at anyone else. He took her arm and began to pull her toward the door. Just before they reached it, from a well of concern that even he did not know he possessed, Lindall Grote spoke across the noiselessness.

"Wait."

Greenleaf stopped, looked around, but said nothing.

"Where are you going with her?"

"It don't concern you."

"Wait. I known Margaret four years. So have most of the other men here. You can damn well bet what happens to her concerns us."

Greenleaf looked around the diner at the men staring intently at their plates of eggs and cups of coffee, then straight at Lindall. "Ayuh. Okay. I was going to ask her to get married."

The customers gaped at each other and Margaret at Greenleaf, astonished, mute as marble statues. Lindall, however, glared at him and spoke.

"That so? All right then. But she ain't got no one to look out for her and Evelyn except us, you know. How old are you?"

"Nineteen."

"How much school did you get?"

"Eighth grade. Then I joined the Army."

"Where'd you serve?"

"The Pacific."

"That where you lost your hand?"

He said nothing and nodded. A wave of approval swept through the audience. Lindall continued, grim and relentless.

"You got a job?"

"I did."

"Well, what happened to it?"

"It was with my father. I just told him this morning I wanted to get married. He told me I was a fool. We had a fight and I walked out."

"Don't he like Margaret?"

"He don't even know her. The bastid. He just don't want me to get married. He don't want to let go of me."

"Well. How you going to support her and her sister?"

"I got some disability from the Army. I'll get work."

The silence returned, broken only when Margaret began to sniff. Finally one of the customers spoke. "Lindall."

"Ayuh."

"Look. We got an opening in the paint shop in the yard. I bet we could get the boy a job there if he wants it."

Everyone looked at Greenleaf. He stood impassively with his back to the door for several seconds; then surprise lit his face and he said, "Why, that would be some nice."

Instantly the restaurant was filled with applause and whistles and cheers. Margaret kissed him and men he did not know clapped him on the back; Lindall came up to him and shook his hand, bellowing out to the customers, "Everybody come back this afternoon after work! Beer's on the house!"

And late, late that night, the well-wishers sent home,

Evelyn (who heard the news of her sister's engagement without the slightest reaction) asleep in the bedroom, they strained together on the floor of the apartment's other room. Margaret held for the first time his stump between her legs, wildly thrusting her pelvis against it, while his puny lust paled and shriveled beside her. There with what may have been a vague presentiment of his father's suicide, the ceremonial arsons, and his two-year imprisonment, he felt his soul shrink from her in sadness. Just for an instant it was all he could do to keep from crying.

4

CLOSED SATURDAY JUNE 4," the sign on Mary's Diner had read all week, although the actual shutdown occurred late the day before. On Friday after the four o'clock shift had let out at the Iron Works, most of the regular customers returned to the restaurant, where crepe paper streamers festooned the ceiling and nosegays of pansies sat in waterglasses upon every table. Some of the men came alone; many brought their wives, who peered nervously about the place, unable to understand what bonds of camaraderie and compassion would obligate their husbands to attend such a bridal dinner. As they entered, the men spoke to Margaret standing alone by the door in a red satin dress and huge red satin bows in her hair.

"Looking great, Mary."

"Ain't you some sharp, dear?"

"Hi, Margaret. How she going?"

She did not speak to any of them, but only smiled numbly, her eyes as brown and glazed as a rind on a baked ham. For two and a half years she had endured her lonely engagement, and now she looked out on the eve of its consummation with emotions both too profound and too confused to permit small talk. So she stood silently ushering in these men, who had spent that same two-and-a-half-year period alternately pitying and attempting to comfort her.

Once inside they mostly went straight to the bar where Lindall Grote was drawing glasses of beer from the worn wood spigot. At one end of the counter sat a basket with a sign beside it, "FOR THE HAPPY COUPLE." Whenever someone tried to pay for a draught, Lindall would direct his attention to the sign.

"That's the cash register, tonight."

"What? Lindall, ain't you feeling well?"

"Christ. He ain't charging for the beer. Somebody better call a doctor. And maybe Digger Perkins" (who ran the largest mortuary in Bath).

While the men drank and joked and wished the couple well, the nervous wives clustered together to talk of their own marriages and their babies and how best to keep their houses clean. Lindall's wife, Bessie, was one of them, as nervous as any, skinnier and noisier than most. Passing among everybody in a snow white dress was Evelyn, her lips pressed tight together, a small, silent, voluptuous, and avenging angel. She carried a tray of hors d'oeuvres. Occasionally a slight motion of her jaw betrayed that she was surreptitiously sampling them, but no one ever saw her put one in her mouth.

At six o'clock almost to the minute Greenleaf walked in, followed by Sheriff and Mrs. Ware. He wore his blue serge prison suit and a white hat with a wide brim. This Margaret lifted from his head; then she kissed his cheek and spoke for the first time since she had appeared downstairs in the red dress. "Alcott. You're here."

From behind him, Sheriff Ware said, "Sure he is. We didn't even have to put the handcuffs on him."

Beneath the burst of laughter Greenleaf murmured, " 'Lo, Margaret," and suddenly he kissed her hard on the mouth. The laughter changed to applause. As he pulled away to face the crowd, he grinned and his eyes glittered; she all at once realized he was drunk.

"Somebody get that boy a beer!" and there was Evelyn in front of him, white and grim as death, with a glass of beer in one hand and the tray of hors d'oeuvres in the other. He took several of these and stuffed them into his mouth. Then, his hand empty, he accepted the foaming glass. For a long moment he chewed vigorously and finally swallowed, washing all down with a gulp of beer. His smile was immutable and wide and terrible, even when his mouth was full of canapés; his eyes were slits beneath his brows and his cheeks were stretched taut—as if eleven hours ago someone had bet him he could not smile continuously from dawn to sunset and he had now almost won. Mute and deaf he stood in the center of the floor, the eye of a small hurricane of people, who swirled and chattered all around him.

"Anybody who puts money on the Red Sox this year is a damn fool."

"Gene, how'd you like to pull beers for a minute?"

"All he done was burn some ice houses down, for Christ's sake. That's why he was in jail."

"Jack deer long enough, you get caught. That's what I say. Oh, hello there, Sheriff."

"You bet, Lin."

"Well, my husband wouldn't pick his pants off the floor if you pointed a gun at him."

"That's what I told him. 'You're a fool,' I said. But he said he got odds."

"Ayuh. Well, I heard something about his father dying or something."

"Frank. Henry. What's up? Early deer season? Ha, ha."

"Damn good, these little critters. Thank you, dear."

"Hell of a spread Lindall's putting out, ain't it?"

"Well, I hope they was good odds. Like a hundred to one."

"Not us, Sheriff. But I hear there's a lot of buck fever over in Lincoln County just now. You been out yet?"

"Naw, the old man himself done that. Strung himself up in the bedroom. The boy come home and found him. Then he went out firing the ice houses. Christ, the sheriff over there's the one who brung him in."

"Anybody interested in a dite to eat?"

From the kitchen behind the bar, fat and sweating, followed by an assistant, Lindall came—lugging two huge steaming kettles that he placed on the counter. Seaweed covered each like green lumpy hair. Pulling it away and tossing it into a trash barrel, he brought from one kettle something large and scarlet, which he arranged on a plate and slid toward the assistant. From the second pot came a clatter of clams, all but extinguishing the shining red flame.

"Look at that, Emmy," said Sheriff Ware.

"There, now. You just mind your manners, Bartholomew. Let the others have a chance before you get in there." Turning to two women, she explained, "He is worse than a hog at Christmas whenever he sees a lobster." Gracefully the sheriff reddened.

"He even looks kind of lobstery, I see," remarked one of the women.

While the guests began a gradual movement toward the bar, cups of melted butter and clam broth were set out on the tables and booths. For a time the noise within the restaurant subsided somewhat as the partygoers feasted. At a table in front of the bar sat the principals: the Wares, the Grotes, and between them Margaret, Evelyn, and Greenleaf—the three as bright and as brave as Old Glory in their several colors of red, white, and blue.

Of the trio only Evelyn ate much. She cracked and sucked at her lobster intently until it was a husk of broken shells. Then she whispered, "Give me yours," to Margaret, who sat in a sacred daze beside her. When there was no response, she reached over her arm and exchanged plates. Greenleaf, still wearing that inexorable smile, picked unsteadily at the pile of clams in front of him and gulped at successive glasses of beer. At last there came the tinging sound of a fork being rapped against a glass, and Sheriff Ware stood up.

"Ladies and gentlemen. Glad to see so many of you here tonight for this happy occasion. And before I say another word, I want to thank—" here he consulted a small page of notes—"Thomas Merryman and Ed Wyman for these lobsters. They took a dreadful chance bringing in so many shorts, and we sure are grateful." (The audience laughed with delight; not one of the lobsters had weighed less than two pounds.) "Also Peter Cook brought the clams. I think these fellows deserve a nice hand."

The crowd clapped and whistled. At last he faced his palms toward them. "Now, my wife tells me that the best man is supposed to make a toast to the bride and groom. I don't know that every one of you will agree with me, but I am the best man at this party. I know it because young Alcott here told me I was.

"So here I am. I got to make this toast, you see, and the only toast I ever made before was to spread jam onto. Ha, ha. But I guess I'm stuck with the job. So what I'd like to do is say something about weddings and why I'm so pleased about this one."

The sheriff paused and looked at the ceiling. When he

spoke again, his voice was quiet and distant, like that of an elderly judge.

"Sooner or later everybody's got to settle down. Got to. I remember my father telling me that before I got married, and it's as true now as then. Nobody can tomcat all their life and not get their head blown off at last. Not that that was about to happen to our Alcott, but what I mean is that a man does need a wife to keep him pointed down the right track.

"Another thing is children. Now, I ain't saying that it's impossible to have children without getting married first—there's a couple of damn-fool kids we got up in Lincoln County right now who found that out just a week ago—but being married does seem to make the little cuffers a lot more welcome when they arrive. I can truly say that it has always been a great regret to Mrs. Ware and myself that we never had children.

"The last thing I got to say about marriage—the truest and most important thing I know—is that a man and wife together can stand up against the world, and that the faith and love of a good woman can make any man unbeatable. What's more, I wouldn't be surprised—though I can't speak from my own experience, of course—that a man's love can have exactly the same effect on a woman." He smiled down at his wife.

"I've known Alcott for a couple of years now. They've been rough ones for him, but he seems to have come through them just fine. I can't think of any boy that deserves all these rewards as much as him. And I tell you, from what I can see, he couldn't have made a better choice than Margaret. I think she is the real goods.

"So, anyway, I guess all that is left is to wish Alcott and Margaret a long and happy marriage, with a fat baby or two tossed in for good measure. Let's drink to them both." He raised his glass of beer in salute, then drank it down.

An instant of silence while everyone followed suit and then the din broke within the diner—whistling, clapping, stomping of feet. The sheriff sat down. The cries started up: "Speech! Speech!"

Slowly and unsteadily, the stump and the one hand pressing against the table, Greenleaf rose, that terrible unwavering smile stretched across his face like rubber. When he was erect, he lifted his arms and crossed them over his chest. Before he could open his mouth to speak, however, his knees buckled; and he slid gently, still smiling, to the floor.

5

AT dawn the next day Margaret was still awake, flat on her back staring at the ceiling, listening to the gentle breathing of her sister beside her in the other bed. The night before, the sheriff had tried to reassure her as he carried Greenleaf to the car. "Don't you worry none, dear. He's just had a dite too much beer, and that ain't lethal. We'll take him home with us and bring him back tomorrow in time for the ceremony, or I'll hand in my badge. Why, I ain't never yet lost a man I was escorting. And I have escorted quite a few of them."

As she lay there, panicked virgin on the morning of her nuptials, soft sweet snores from her sister singing her a prothalamion, she fretted over the future. Questions assaulted her: would the gracious bridegroom appear in time and place appointed? Would the unrehearsed wedding actually occur? Would she at last be deflowered? bear children? live happily ever after? She ran her hands over her cotton nightshirt, feeling the body beneath. There was no response; her fingers might have been exploring dead flesh. They came finally to her empty and rigid crotch. She forced herself to remember past humpings with Greenleaf and, when even these failed to warm her, pressed herself further to the limits of her sexual imagination—phantasmagoric ruttings of rams and stallions and great bull elephants mad with must, all half seen and half felt, all interspersed with the flickering vision of Greenleaf's handless forearm driving with great strength up and into her body. Heat burst within her. With a moan she rolled over in the bed, her fingers pushing into her vagina, and buried her head in the pillow to stifle the cries that came bursting out from someplace deep inside her, spatterings from a cauldron. Beside her, Evelyn stirred but did not wake. Her passion peaked, she sobbed, and sudden sleep enveloped her.

The next thing she knew, sunlight was streaming into her eyes and Evelyn was hissing into her ear: "Margaret. You old cow. Wake up."

"Wha— what time is it?"

"Past ten. Get up."

She rushed from bed to the bathroom where she drew a hot tub, the first in a series of steps designed to transform her from Cinderella to princess. For more than an hour she washed, dried, brushed, powdered, and rouged. At eleven thirty she adjourned for lunch, such as it was—two slices of toast and coffee in the empty restaurant—then she stumped back upstairs where she dentifriced, lipsticked, mascaraed, plucked a few stray hairs from between her eyebrows, and donned shining new silky underwear, her best girdle, new nylon hose, and petticoats;

over which (with the sulky assistance of her sister) went the gown—Ah!—of white satin, floor length, yoked and long sleeved, cut and pinned and stitched *à main* through the long nights of Greenleaf's incarceration; the white satin shoes, three inches in heel, *garni* with silk orange petals; and finally the veil, white tulle, dropping to the middle of her back: incarnation of Hymen, of modest virginity on the threshold of surrender.

Ahead of the pink-frocked Evelyn, gracefully and nervously she tripped down the stairs to where the Grotes waited to take them to the church. Bessie Grote was the first to speak: "Margaret, you are just beautiful. Lindall, look at her."

"Sweet Jesus. Fabulous, simply fabulous. Look like a queen."

"Well, dear, don't just stand there with your mouth open. You've got something for Margaret, don't you?"

"Why, ayuh. That's right. Here you go." He thrust at her a bouquet of red roses.

"Oh, Lin. They are so lovely. Thank you. Thank you both." Tears welled in her eyes; she quickly leaned toward him and kissed his cheek.

Evelyn spoke sharply, a knife snapping across softening butter. "Come on, Margaret. Let's go."

And all the way to the West Bath Baptist Church, Margaret cradled her left ring finger in her right hand and kept her gaze in her lap, silently begging the surly gods for this, the one last small miracle.

6

At the church the sheriff and Greenleaf were waiting in a small room in the front just to the right of the altar. They had been there nearly twenty minutes, speaking seldom and then in hushed tones, mostly listening to the drone of the organ and the faint conversation of the arriving congregation.

Finally the minister came up a flight of stairs into the room to join them. He was a smallish man with wizened features and great round spectacles, which gave him the aspect of an angry owl. Greenleaf had met him once before with Margaret. His name was Reverend Mank.

"I must say," he said in precise, pedantic tones, "I don't much care for a wedding without prior rehearsal. Are you certain you can remember everything I have told you?"

"Yes, sir," whispered Greenleaf, all but inaudible. He was dressed exactly as he had been the night before, except that Sheriff Ware had stuck a white carnation in his lapel.

"Very well. The bride has arrived. Are we set?" Reverend Mank pressed a button next to the door jamb and instantly the organ music ceased. "Come along," he said and, opening the door, stepped into the transept. The sheriff gently pushed Greenleaf after him.

The organist swung forte into Wagner's "Bridal Chorus." From the rear of the church came a flash of bright pink and then Greenleaf saw Evelyn, white faced and furious, sailing down the aisle toward them. Behind her, on the right arm of Lindall Grote, progressed the bride: tall and white and regal, the red fire of the roses held with both hands at her waist, face demure inside the veil with eyes downcast, transfigured, bathed with some kind of holy light, so that Greenleaf thought in a flash, No, it ain't Margaret, no woman that looked like that would ever marry me, and all at once they were even in a row with Margaret rising white and straight as a steeple above the other four and the minister stooped over them all like a hawk, now speaking.

"Dearly beloved, holy and happy is the hour, glorious and good is the day, when a man and a woman are bound together in the blessed contract of matrimony. In this hour on this day the two persons here—Alcott and Margaret—come forth so to bind themselves together."

It seemed to Greenleaf that the minister spoke from a great distance; yet when he heard his name pronounced, he shuddered. Reverend Mank continued: "Marriage is an honorable and sacred estate. It was instituted by God Jehovah, who created Eve from the rib of Adam and commanded them, our first parents, to be fruitful and multiply. It was confirmed by Jesus Christ, who blessed a wedding in Galilee with his presence and there transformed water into wine. Finally, it was commended by Saint Paul, who compared it to Christ's loving relationship with the Church and extolled it as a means toward living a sinless life." He paused.

"Who gives Margaret to be married to Alcott?"

"I do," said Lindall Grote promptly. Then he scuttled to the nearest pew and sat beside his wife.

"The rewards of marriage are great, as are its responsibilities. You both must be prepared to provide each other support in adversity as well as to rejoice in each other's successes." Here Reverend Mank glared out over the congregation fiercely, as if he dared anyone to dispute his words. When nobody did, he looked down at Greenleaf.

"Do you, Alcott, take Margaret to be your lawful wedded wife? Will you honor and cherish her, love and sustain her, in sickness and in health, in poverty and in wealth, for better or for worse, devoutly promising to be everlastingly true to her until death do you part?"

Greenleaf's eyes were blank. He looked straight ahead and did not move. The minister said, "Answer, 'I do.' "

Sheriff Ware nudged him. "Hah? Oh. Ayuh. I do."

Reverend Mank repeated the vows to Margaret, whose reply was firm and harsh and loud. "I do." From the congregation came an audible sob, followed by assorted sniffs and throat clearings.

Then came the blessing and presentation of the ring, and a prayer. The minister pronounced them man and wife, and their Rubicon was behind them. The service was almost finished—all that remained were the kiss, the recessional to Mendelssohn's "Wedding March," and the confetti-and-rice shower outside. As Reverend Mank was speaking, Greenleaf found that he had become perfectly attuned to the sights, sounds, and smells around him, aware of his surroundings in the way a dying man might suddenly start to register everything he is about to leave behind. He felt his collar pressing against his neck, heard the assembly snuffling. The minister's voice rang out, each of his words marking Greenleaf's consciousness like branding irons: "Whom God hath joined together let no man put asunder."

There was then a sound, distinct, a snort of laughter; and Greenleaf snapped his gaze past his new wife's head to confront the scornful derision of his new sister-in-law, who even now with increasing stridency and volume and mounting hysteria before that company (to the horror and chagrin of the bride, the minister, the groom, and the entire company itself) laughed. And laughed.

IV Home

Domus sua cuique tutissimum refugium. —Pandects
Oh! Dulce, dulce domum! —George Nugent Reynolds
Where we love is home. —Oliver Wendell Holmes
East and West, Home is best. —Charles Haddon Spurgeon
Be it ever so humble, there's no place like home. —John Howard Payne
Home is home, though it be ever so homely. —John Clarke
It is for homely features to keep home, They had their name thence.
—John Milton
Give me a home, where the buffalo roam. —Brewster Higley
It takes a heap o' livin' in a house t' make it home. —Edgar A. Guest
In fact there was but one thing wrong with the Babbitt house: it was not a home. —Sinclair Lewis
A House is not a Home. —Polly Adler
Home is where one starts from. —T. S. Eliot
Home is the place where, when you have to go there, They have to take you in. —Robert Frost
Home is the girl's prison and the woman's workhouse. —George Bernard Shaw
"The Old Folks at Home" —Stephen Foster
"Home for Christmas" —Norman Rockwell
Old Folks' Home; Sailors' Home; Soldiers' Home; Home of the Inebriate; The Home for Confirmed Invalids; Dr. Bernardo's Homes for Orphan Waifs; homes for wayward girls, for the emotionally disturbed, for the mentally infirm.
Home plates, home runs, home rule, home brew.
Funeral homes.
Nice people come from nice homes. —Patricia Guinan

1

In the beginning, the changes in his life were legion. He could not begin to list them all as they spun down around and dizzied him like bright autumn leaves swirling in the wind. At times it seemed he would drown in them: the kisses, the kindnesses, the meals, the made beds, the adornments to person and place, the sounds and smells, the softness, the warmth. Yet, within these strictures which constituted his new life Greenleaf felt an illusion of freedom—freedom at least from the forces which had shaped his old one.

It seemed that he had before always been directed toward ends too remote and too immense for him to comprehend: the destruction of Japanese forces during the war, or more recently the manufacture of Maine license plates while in prison. Now he felt he lived for himself and his new family, deliberately, supporting them only because he chose to do so, only because he had singled them out as objects of his support. Although he did not articulate these feelings even to himself, he believed himself confronted—for the first time in his experience—with recognizable free choice. Small wonder he was at first flustered.

Small wonder indeed. No one had ever before looked to him as a source of welfare or come to him as a matter of course for advice. When Margaret asked him for grocery money or consulted him about new curtains in the living room, he felt weak and harried, but at the same time illuminated by vague distinction. He who had never been exposed to domesticity in his life now found himself precisely in the center of it. It was heady wine.

So, baffled by home, he retreated, went back to work. Before the wedding he had got the old wrecker going (actually, it was one he and his father had built from an old Chevrolet after the crash in front of Mary's Diner three years ago, when he had met Margaret) and had started gathering up scrap metal for sale. Now he began to build a garage/workshop for his automotive work. With his own hand he graded, formed, and poured a cement floor twelve feet by twenty-four, then set about the walls and the roof.

Meanwhile, Margaret threw herself into homemaking. Cobwebs disappeared. Curtains went up on every window, even the one in the outhouse. Paint dried on the kitchen and bedroom walls; floors shone with unaccustomed wax. The weeds in front of the house fell before her sickle, and the culch and clutter both in and immediately outside the house yielded to her importunity. However, with the exception of clearing a small garden plot, she did not attempt to deal with the great accretion of junk that lay all about the house—a legacy of the late Eustis, her would-have-been father-in-law. (She had quickly discovered that Eustis had left behind other legacies besides the junk outside. After all, he had lived in the house too long not to color it with his own saturnine hues, and sometimes it seemed that her experiments in homemaking consisted entirely of erasing the old man's aesthetic signature.)

One day she turned her attention to the front room, armed with a fistful of grubby old *Better Homes and Gardens* and *House Beautiful*s. She had previously washed and waxed its floor and hung blue curtains over its windows, but now she looked long upon it with a careful and critical eye. It was eight feet wide and fourteen long, pine-paneled, with a wood stove and a brick chimney at the end. Over the mantel hung an object that she had at first taken for some kind of hunting trophy. Now she saw that it was the lower half of a human leg, complete with skeletal foot, bleached bones, and dust, wired together and mounted on a three-foot piece of stained walnut. Once recognized, this display affronted her so much that she decided immediately to remove it. She had at this time been married more than three weeks.

She approached the leg warily and reached up to the

mounting board. It was nailed into the wall, and though there was a niche in back of part of it where she could slip her fingers, she could not move it. Greenleaf was outside hammering something, so she went out to him.

"Alcott."

"Hey."

"What are you making now?" He was spiking together two-by-fours.

"These here will be the walls."

She watched him set a spike with his hand, slamming it into the wood so it stood perfectly perpendicular, start it with two careful taps of the hammer, and drive it home with four more strong ones. "Well, won't that be nice?"

"Ayuh." He paused, looked at her. "What are you up to, Queenie?"

"Oh. That's right. I'm decorating the living room. Can you come in and help me with something?"

"Sure."

"Bring your hammer."

She turned for the house, her heart full to the bursting, her young husband following the swish of her cotton dress. Once inside she pointed. "There. That."

"The stove? What's wrong with it?"

"No. *That.* The leg." From the kitchen Margaret's radio—a large Philco table model she had owned for years and had brought with her when she married—was distantly playing strange music: "On the Mis-sis-sis-sis-sis-sis-sis-sis-sin-a-wah."

"Hah?"

"Look at it, Alcott. It just don't fit in with my decor. See this picture here." She held a magazine in front of him. "I want to hang a bric-a-brac shelf like that one there."

He considered. "You can put your bric-a-brac shelf between the windows just as good."

"Well, sure I can. But you won't want smelly old bones in your living room, do you?"

"They never smelled before."

"You want them to stay?"

"Hell, Margaret. It was my old man's leg. We always hung it there."

"But, honey, he didn't want us to get married. He didn't want you to leave home or nothing. Remember? He was a bastid. You said so. Lots of times." Her lip trembled.

He glared at her, then turned and stomped out the door. "There is someone who waits for me," sang the radio. Margaret stood stunned, a storm of distress gathering in her face. Before it could break, however, a shiny Cadillac pulled into the yard, distracting her. It contained Lindall and Bessie Grote and in the back seat Evelyn. Margaret stepped outside to greet the arrivals, her agitation dissolving in her pleasure at seeing them.

"How's the honeymooners?" shouted Lindall, hopping out of the car. "Still honeymooning?"

"We ain't doing too bad," said Greenleaf amiably and went up to shake his hand.

"Well, I always say, the honeymoon ain't over till you start going to bed when you're tired and getting up when you're not."

Margaret blushed and Bessie snapped at him. "You just watch out for yourself, Lindall Grote. There ain't no need of that. How are you, dear?"

"Fine, Bessie," said Margaret. "And here's Evelyn. You been behaving yourself at the Grotes'?"

Evelyn said nothing. She was dressed in scuffed loafers,

white socks, loose blue jeans with the legs rolled up to mid-calf, and a man's white shirt, the tails of which luffed like a jib in the summer breeze.

"Course she has."

"Come in and see what I'm doing in the house," said Margaret to the females.

"Oh, I'd love to."

Evelyn looked around bleakly; then the three went inside.

The men stood for a moment savoring the silence left by their passage. The warm sunlight fell down around them and the yard: daisies and grasses and clover, growing high and thick, wildly framing each aggregation of decaying metal like an art gallery—mottled green ragged mats laid over renditions of auto hoods and bedsprings, all of these the same soft, rich, patient reddish brown. Then Lindall noticed the hammered two-by-fours and went over to inspect them. "What you got here, Alcott?"

"Putting up a shop. My old man used to run a used parts business. Like on the sign out front. Thought I'd get it going again. Rebuild some old motors, maybe whole cars, out of scrap. Do some repair work, too."

"Sounds pretty good." Involuntarily, very slightly, he winced as he saw his Cadillac shining like a single jewel in this landscape covered with dented and rusted fenders. Then his eyes fell on the blue Pontiac by the house, which despite its battered nose and patriotic mottoes did not look all that bad: the windows were intact, the axle blocked up so that the wheels hung off the ground, the roof and sides nearly unblemished, and the interior still plush; all of which served to inspire some vague hope rather than the definite despair of the rest of Greenleaf's stock, so Lindall addressed himself to it. "Looks like that one could be fixed up pretty good."

He almost smiled. "I suppose. But I don't guess I want to. Not that one."

"That right? Be worth your while, wouldn't it?"

"Oh, ayuh. But first it was kind of a birthday present from my old man. Then when I went into the Army, he decorated it with them sayings. I guess I'll just leave it alone."

"Sure." Lindall paused. "Say. I thought you didn't get along too good with your father."

"That's right. I didn't."

Lindall walked over to study the Pontiac more closely. He opened the door and leaned in. Dust rose in clouds from the upholstery when he clapped the seat. Then he turned around and sat, his right arm hooking over the steering wheel. With Greenleaf regarding him soberly, he began to speak, his gaze directed somewhere in the vicinity of his shoe tips.

"Yes, sir, I think you two can have a fine life together out here. I wish you all the luck in the world. . . . Course, it'll be a lot of work. If there's anything Bessie or I can do . . ." He trailed off. Then he looked up and his voice was low and hurried.

"Alcott, one thing. Watch out for that Evelyn. She's a nasty little bitch. I hate to say anything about her because she's Margaret's sister, but she is poison."

"Well, she does seem a dite independent sometimes."

"Something more than a dite. I've known her since she was ten or eleven, and I seen her pull some ugly little stunts in that time. Nothing big, mind you, but small stuff like stealing tip money from Margaret or breaking things on purpose. Margaret tried to get her a job washing dishes in the restaurant once, but she broke so many I had to haul her right out of there. The morning after that, I found a turd laying on the floor of the ladies' room. Christ. I was sure she done it, but I couldn't see how to prove it."

The words came faster. "I think she's a little nuts, myself. The way she carried on at your wedding. You know, the minute you two got out of that church, she just shut up like a stone."

"She give you any trouble this past month?"

"None to speak of. She ain't around very much. I got no idea where the hell she goes. I do know she hasn't been happy with us, but she's never happy anyways. We took her to the movies last week. *Song of the South.* You know, about Uncle Remus and the rabbit and all?"

Greenleaf shook his head.

"It's funny, parts of it. About a nigger slave in the South who tells stories about a rabbit. Some of it's cartoons and some ain't. A real family picture. Well, after we get out, Bessie asks her how she liked it. She says she wished she could live back then. 'Why?' says Bessie. 'So I could buy me a slave,' she says. 'If you got a slave, you tell them what to do and they got to do it. If they don't, you can whip them.' Goddamn. She scares me.

"I don't know. She's seventeen now, or almost. Maybe she needs a boyfriend. Might straighten her out. But, Christ—what a life, to be the boyfriend. Jesus!

"Anyways, we thought maybe you was ready now to take her back." He finished in a great rush of words.

"Sure. We been expecting her any time."

"Oh. Great." He expelled a long gentle breath. "Say, Alcott. What do you think of the Red Sox? Won eleven of their last twelve games! And last Friday against the Browns—twenty-two to two! Great stuff, eh? Maybe we're in for another 1946."

"Jesus," said Greenleaf truthfully, "I hope not."

Lindall stepped out of the Pontiac and the two men walked together up to the house. And when the Grotes were about to leave, about an hour or so later, Evelyn removed two paper shopping bags filled with her belongings—one of clothing, the other entirely of movie magazines—from the back seat of the Cadillac and carried them into the smaller bedroom, where she was to live.

So now they were three. At first Greenleaf scarcely noticed the difference, while he and Margaret turned to their patterns of building and making. Between breakfasts and suppers he hardly saw either of them. Alone in the yard he spent days in a frenzy, wrestling with creatures of wood and metal, throwing them and being thrown, as he raised three walls and a roof or tore the metallic guts from recent and prewar wrecks. Whenever he got working on a car, his face took on the expression of a frantic terrier trying to dismember and bury a dead bear; the parts he worried from the engine and chassis would pop onto the ground like bones. Miraculously, they would somehow remain in usable condition, and soon he began to realize some profit: a garage in Wiscasset took several salvage parts from him and asked him to try to dig up some others. After work, he would return to the house to wash the grease from his hand and face, eat his supper, and relax with his wife in his newly decorated living room—a perfect puppy of domestic bliss.

Margaret felt her sister's presence more than Greenleaf. For one thing, the bonds of consanguinity could well be expected to make the one more aware of the spirit of the other. But there was another reason: the two were thrust together in the house for most of each day, and for Margaret it was an oppressive juxtaposition. Out here in the country, cut off from the diversity of Bath, Evelyn had nowhere to go—no shops, no crowds, no movies, no retreat at all—so she was forced to stay home. She did not care to be alone in the woods; her antisociality was the sort that had to be reinforced by having people around her. She displayed the disposition not of a hermit but of an assassin.

The second night after her arrival Margaret had spoken to Greenleaf as they lay side by side in bed. "I don't know what to do. She won't talk to me. I can't get her to say a word. She just lays around all morning looking at those movie magazines and listening to my radio. I finally told her to take the radio and the magazines into her room if all she was going to do was mope. But even in there she gets on my nerves."

"Huh. Well, give her a little time." He reached over and cupped his hand over her enflanneled breast.

"What you want." She giggled.

"You can give me a little time too." Then they were pressing silently together in the darkness until soft flesh parts and quick thrusts came quickly and they parted, parts soft and moist and warm, and soon slept, apart.

They had not, however, solved the problem of Evelyn, who for three days did not utter a word. At meals Greenleaf and Margaret would try to draw her out by talking to her, but she ignored them, staring at her mute grubby fingers. Finally, though, the strain of maintaining this wall of silence wore her down, must have done so, for she was at last moved to speak.

It was suppertime of the third day. Margaret was explaining what she had learned about the coming Independence Day celebration to be held in Wiscasset: "The postmistress says there's a parade right down Main Street in the afternoon and fireworks over the river at night. They get the American Legion band and a drum-and-bugle corps from someplace to march in it. The Veterans of Foreign Wars wants Alcott to be in it too, but he says he won't. That right, honey?"

"Ayuh."

"But anyways, we can all go into Wiscasset and watch the parade. Then we'll have a picnic supper and watch the fireworks. Don't that sound like fun?"

Greenleaf took a biscuit from a plateful in front of him. He split it with his thumb and, holding it like a pair of clamshells, scooped up a pat of butter between the halves. Then he wiped it in some honey on his plate and stuffed it into his mouth. "Goddamn, Margaret, them biscuits are some good."

"Now, you shouldn't try to talk with your mouth full."

"The Grotes got a television set," said Evelyn suddenly, bitterly.

There was silence as they all weighed the apparent injustice of this fact. Then Greenleaf said, "That so?"

When Evelyn did not respond, Margaret said, "I didn't know that. They must have just got it. Did you watch it, Evelyn?"

She nodded. "I seen lots of things."

"That so? What were they?" asked Greenleaf.

"Lots of things," she snapped. "Movies. Newsreels. Comedies. Just like going to the movie theater."

"No kidding," said Margaret.

"Sure. I seen one show about some nigger slaves down South. One of them was called Uncle Recess. He told stories about a talking rabbit. And a fox. Television. It's better than a goddamned radio, you bet."

Greenleaf drew a breath and faced her, his voice gentle but firm. "What are you talking about, sissy? You're telling a bigger story than Uncle Recess ever did. Lindall told me about that movie. And he said that him and Bessie took you to the theater to see it. Lindall ain't got a television."

Evelyn's face stiffened and grew dark. She clamped her

mouth shut. Around the table all motion and sound stopped for perhaps five seconds, perhaps five years. Then the tableau broke apart, as she jumped up and rushed to her bedroom. The door slammed shut.

"Oh, Alcott. Why'd you say that? Maybe she just forgot that Uncle Recess was a movie. Got mixed up."

"The Grotes ain't got a television."

"They don't? How do you know that? Did Lin tell you?"

"Nope. But there ain't any stations in Maine. Sheriff Ware was telling me about wanting to get a television one time, but he said that the nearest stations was up to Boston. So you can't look at nothing on a television in Maine."

He paused as a tremendous crash let go within Evelyn's closed room. Then came a regular banging noise, against the floor perhaps, as of a hammer. Both hurried to the bedroom door, Greenleaf threw it open, and there she was: kneeling on the floor beside tiny bits and pieces of Margaret's Philco—splinters and shards of cabinet and tubes—even now raising over her head an object he immediately recognized as his dead father's artificial leg, bringing it down to the floor, atomizing more thoroughly the mess before her.

They quieted her, and while Margaret got her undressed and in bed, Greenleaf removed the prosthesis to the rear of his closet. Neither he nor Margaret afterward alluded to this scene in any way; however, on July 14 he brought home to his family a new Capehart television set, mahogany-cabineted with a nine-inch screen, which could do nothing but sit blankly in the front room until 1952 when channels 6, 13, and 53 in Portland would begin their broadcast operations. Three weeks after the arrival of this miraculous creature, Margaret introduced the prospect of another—this the zenith of their joint homemaking efforts—by announcing that she believed herself pregnant.

2

MARY Newell was born in 1870 or so near what is now Old Town, the daughter to Susup Newell and granddaughter to the old chief himself, Kctiwabu. In time she became the last remaining child of the Matagwesu family of the Penobscots, "People of the White Rocks," one of the two principal tribes of Maine Indians. Her memory encompassed a great span of years and two worlds: first her childhood among the Matagwesu, also called the Wabu—"Rabbits"—a wretched tribe, who existed mostly thanks to the charity of other, wealthier, families and whose patriarch was named Kctiwabu—"Old Rabbit"—because he limped; and later her adult life among the whites, French and Anglo, trappers, farmers, and merchants. Both worlds were filthy and squalid and poor, the former characterized by hunger and deprivation, the latter by hunger and abuse. She wandered from beatings to rapes to once the witnessing of a murder, somehow surviving them all until finally about 1920 she washed up on the shores of the Sheepscot, some hundred miles and several thousand pains from her tribal home.

She acquired a deserted log cabin in the woods near North Whitefield where she created out of lore and superstition and good luck a sort of practice in midwifery and forest medicine. She had learned much about suffering in her life, which may have been why she was so well equipped to deal with it. By the end of her first five years in the Whitefield area she had assisted over a hundred humans into the world, generally with success. In 1926 Greenleaf himself had felt before any other sensation her hand upon his shining legs and rump; and although he could not be expected to recall her rough handling or his indignant response, Mary could, that and more: the pale thin-faced frightened woman; her husband, dour and impatient, who stumped up and down the front room throughout the delivery; the slippery infant feet signaling a breech; the quick blood, the birth and death. It was not her fault. Her reputation as midwife was already secure enough to absorb the loss of the mother, and besides, the father had been appeased by the gift of a son.

So she had aged and shrunk and her face shriveled into leathery creases and her black eyes sank deeper into her head. She seldom spoke. When she did, people had difficulty understanding much of her queer hoarse patois. Most believed her a trifle mad, but with a sacred insanity—the holiness of fools—and they still went to her. In the fall of 1949, then, Greenleaf brought his pregnant wife to her cabin for a prenatal consultation.

They found her sitting on a chair outside her cabin, smoking a pipe in the September sunshine with her eyes closed. A long cotton dress covered her body from neck to wrist to ankle. Her iron-gray hair was tucked up into a bun, a few iron-gray wisps floating at her nape like feathery cobwebs. On her feet were scuffed G.I. boots, small enough to fit her, perhaps, but so massive in proportion to her antique frailty that Greenleaf wondered for an instant if she could actually lift them in order to walk.

"Mary," he said as they approached.

Her eyelids snapped open. "Kii."

"It's Alcott Greenleaf. From down the Wiscasset Road. Remember? You tended my mother and nursed me when she died."

"Aha." She nodded.

"This here's my wife. Margaret. She's going to have a baby."

Mary got up slowly, the while staring at Margaret, her

black eyes bright and deep in her face. "Aha. Bien. Come in house."

They followed her into the close, rank cabin. In the dim light they could see that they were surrounded by rummage: boxes of cards and paper, pictures, animal skins, small pieces of furniture, dried herbs and leaves, piles of knickknacks and geegaws—like the apartment of a highly successful packrat. She led them to the rear, where four chairs were arranged about a warm wood stove as if around a table. "Abi," she said, indicating where they should sit.

Then she reached down beside the stove and lifted a black medical bag, worn and cracked. Setting it on the chair next to Margaret, she selected from within it an object wrapped in white linen, which, unwrapped, sparkled like silver in the shadows. "Have inst'ments, me. Clean. Mine." She patted Margaret's shoulder encouragingly. As she sat down, she asked, "When come baby? Many month?"

"In the spring," answered Margaret.

"Aha. Bien. Ha, ha. No hurry. Come back in spring, when you get big. Ha, ha." She rolled her hands over her lap, defining an imaginary fetus. Then she looked past Margaret to Greenleaf. "Ay you, eh? Give her whatever she ask for. Ever'thing. Not to mark the baby."

Margaret spoke very carefully and softly, looking down at her lap. "Why'd Mrs. Greenleaf die?"

"Kii. She ver' sick. Weak. Eee. He breech."

"Oh."

"Not to worry. You have a strong baby, you."

Margaret managed a smile. "Ayuh."

And that was that. She and Greenleaf left quickly, bursting into the fresh air and sunshine as if they themselves were together birthing. Mary watched them go. Smiling a gap-toothed smile, she turned back into the cabin, back to the stove, where she moved a kettle over the fire.

Without warning her memory leaped to a moment more than fifty years gone: a greeting dance when her poor pathetic family of Rabbits had once visited the Awesus family—the "Bears"—whose wealth and strength was beyond the comprehension of most of the Wabu and certainly out of the reach of them all. Mary had been a pretty girl, though bony (indeed, few from her family were fat); and the leader of the Awesus, Chief Denis Mitchell, had noticed her—had honored her by inviting her to dance the shawl. She and an Awesus girl had danced with men from each other's tribes, wearing bright silk scarves over their heads. After a bit the girls covered also the heads of whichever partner they most favored; these men were thus chosen to be their sweethearts for the remainder of the visit. Mary had selected a strong, handsome *skinos,* who was so attentive and kind to her while the Wabu stayed that she had hated to leave him; still, this was her happiest memory from life among her people. Now that she was grown old, it came on her from time to time, unbidden, always leaving her breathless.

In the dim cabin her booted feet began a stiff shuffle. Her hoarse voice gasped, then began to croak the ancient song of feasts and drunken lovers:

For perhaps ten minutes she danced on, tripping in and among the shades of her lost people.

3

CHRISTMAS! Noël! Hallelujah! The season of winter joy, new years, hopes and fears, came storming upon them like a chorus of herald angels singing. For Greenleaf it might as well have been his first; he had never before had occasion to observe the holiday. His father had been left indifferent, his fellow G.I.'s despondent, his prison mates largely cynical, by Christmases past. Now possessing a family, he found himself ready and anxious to celebrate the present one for them.

His plans for its observance were strictly secular—decorations, gifts, a big dinner. No churches for him, though he not only understood that Christmas was a religious holiday commemorating the birth of God's only son but moreover approved of it as such, somehow reckoning that the birth of a divine son would demand at least as much rejoicing as that of his own mortal one would. (Without ever mentioning aloud the sex of his unborn child, he inevitably thought of it as male.) So he bought a wreath, wrappings, presents for both women, and a twenty-three-pound turkey.

The family had settled down considerably during autumn. He himself had taken a job for the winter at a garage in Wiscasset called Tuttle's. Evelyn, who in September refused to enter Wiscasset High School, rode with him to town to a restaurant, the Busy Bee, where she waited on a counter and several tables with as little effort and as much effect as possible, making easily ten dollars a day in tips. (The restaurant owner suffered her petulance and indolence willingly when he saw that she attracted male customers like flies to honey and that her quick scorn toward all of them kept them turning their pockets inside out so that they could remain there, sipping coffee, dunking doughnuts, and watching the foxy twitch of her haunches or the quiver of her sharp nipples through the white uniform she wore.) She paid Margaret twenty-five dollars a month for room and board, which by tacit agreement freed her to come and go without restriction.

So it was not long before she began to go out with grown men, passing by altogether the familiar adolescent rites of courtship, with proms and fluffy dresses and bubble gum and tragedies of broken dates or acne eruptions, arriving directly at the severe realities beyond them. The men who pulled into Greenleaf's yard one or several nights a week and sat in their cars honking for her to come out were his age and older, a rough, boisterous lot—maybe not the equal of most prisoners at Thomaston, but not by much their inferiors either. They never called her on the telephone, but made their appointments somehow during her days at work. Greenleaf and Margaret never met them, for she never brought them in to be introduced, but he heard from scuttlebutt around Wiscasset who some of them were: truck drivers, drifters, a few sailors from the naval base in Brunswick, one of the local firemen. They drove cars and gave her money, and they all danced around her like chained bears.

Least happy among the family was Margaret. This surprised him (and would have surprised Evelyn also, had she bothered to think about it), for Margaret all her life had been so easily pleased, so willing to accept whatever fate was cast for her. It was difficult for him to tell what was bothering her because even now she so seldom complained, but he could sense the loneliness and depression hanging over her like a pall. These he put down to her daily isolation while he and Evelyn were at work, coupled with her discomfort in pregnancy. Morning sickness, cramps, and dizziness forced her to spend most of the day in bed, miserable and tired; and at night she could not sleep. Vaguely he hoped that this, their first Christmas together, would bring about some small miracle by which she would be granted a measure of peace.

When Evelyn climbed into the pickup sometime after four o'clock on Christmas Eve, she had to settle in among several large cardboard cartons. "What's all this stuff?"

He grinned at her as they pulled away from the curb. "Santa Claus don't go around blabbing what he got to stick in your stocking."

"This stuff's for me?"

"Stay out of it, now. It depends if you been good. I guess you'd be glad to get a sockful of coal."

"Huh."

"No? Well, then. Maybe some of it's for you after all."

She said nothing, only leaned back against the seat. It had snowed that day, was snowing still, and outside the quick winter night was falling. Heavy flakes whipped toward them out of the darkness as they rolled together over the soft white roads, the steady click of the tire chains soothing them like a ticking clock or heartbeats. Evelyn lit a cigarette; the match flared brightly inside the dim cab.

"What you got for Margaret?"

"Uhuh. You got to wait, sissy. You'll see tomorrow."

"Huh." She did not speak or breathe for several seconds. "I got a date tonight."

"That so?"

"We're going to Brunswick to a party. It's with a fellow that's got a black convertible. With whitewall tires and red leather seats. Sometimes he lets me drive it. It goes some fast, you bet."

"Hah. You going to put the top down tonight?"

"He's got a lot of money."

"That so? What's his name?"

"You don't know him. Leslie. Leslie Terror. From Brunswick."

"Leslie Terror? Ha. Say, sissy, why don't you ask him for dinner tomorrow? The Wares and the Grotes are coming up. We're going to have a turkey. We'd like to see Leslie Terror come, fine."

Evelyn sounded doubtful. "I don't know. I'll ask him. I hope Margaret ain't going to puke all over the table."

"Maybe you could help her with the cooking. She ain't been feeling good all fall."

They fell silent. Soon the pickup was rolling through the three or four inches of powdery snow covering Greenleaf's driveway. As they stopped in front of the door, Evelyn said almost to herself, "That damn Leslie better show up tonight"; and then they were out of the truck and inside.

From the door they could see into the bedroom, where Margaret was asleep. The wood stove was out and the house was cold. Greenleaf went into the kitchen to turn on the gas stove. "Goddamn. Sissy, come look at this." Laid upon the table was the food for their Christmas—pumpkin and apple pies; jars of applesauce, bright green beans, and orange carrots; scrubbed potatoes and a squash; and in the center like a massive centerpiece the turkey, pale and stuffed and trussed: the whole seeming to be poised almost like a diver at that hushed instant before he steps to the end of the board and leaps into the air.

"You better get that Leslie Terror to come," said Greenleaf. "We will need some help with all this."

Later, Margaret awakened, supper eaten, Evelyn at last departed to the roars and honks of Leslie's convertible, they sat on the couch in front of the snapping wood stove beneath the bones of Eustis's leg.

"All set for tomorrow?"

She had drawn her legs under her body, hunching up like an ailing rabbit, but she tried to smile as she answered. "Hope so. I got to start the turkey pretty soon."

"Hell, I can get that. How about Santa Claus? You ready for him?"

"Huh? Santa Claus? Oh, Alcott, get along."

He did not reply, only stood up and walked to the front door. She watched him go outside and in less than a minute he was back inside; under his arm was a large cardboard box. He smiled. "Merry Christmas."

"Oh, Alcott." She heaved herself up from the couch and started to come around to meet him. "What is it?"

He stood by a small table between the two front windows and placed the carton on the floor. From it he removed a wooden cabinet, which he set on the table. She took a step toward him, almost tripped over her robe, grabbed the arm on the couch. "What is it?"

He fiddled with an electric cord, turned a knob here, a dial there; and suddenly, magically, Bing Crosby's rich voice filled the room as did the angels the sky when they sang over Bethlehem—"May your days be merry and bright"—and Margaret slowly sank to her knees. "Oh, Alcott. It's so beautiful. Just beautiful."

The new radio caroled them to sleep; and when he stirred the next morning, it was caroling still—this time a program of Christmas music by the Mormon Tabernacle Choir, 375 lusty voices strong—"Glo-o-o-o-o-oria in Excelsis De-e-o!" He stretched over warm pillows, gradually coming awake, feeling first the space of Margaret's absence beside him, then growing into the cold air of the bedroom.

And then he was up and the house was alive and miraculously joyous: Margaret smiling in the kitchen, wearing red ribbons in her hair (for the first time since last summer), gently bumping her stomach against the stove as she roasted and baked and simmered; Evelyn smiling in the living room, gloating over a new white sweater and silver jewelry; Greenleaf smiling everywhere, playing Santa Claus, building up the fire, doing jobs for Margaret. As the morning progressed, he was even able to induce Evelyn to help. They cleaned up the living room and put the table near the wood stove, arranging chairs around it and knives, forks, and spoons on top of it. The new radio sang in the background: "God rest ye merry, gentlemen, let nothing ye dismay." For a while they hummed with it; then Evelyn spoke.

"This is how Christmas is supposed to be, ain't it?"

"How do you mean?"

"All them songs, and a big dinner, and presents."

"I guess."

"I never had one before."

"We had one in the Army. I was in the Pacific and we got special rations—canned ham and sweet potatoes—and the loudspeaker played a couple of Christmas songs. And we all got presents from the Red Cross. I got a pair of mittens." He looked down at his stump. "Real handy. Ha. Course, I had two hands then, but still it didn't never get below sixty in the shade, so I didn't get much of a chance to use them mittens."

"Oh, Christmas tree, oh, Christmas tree," sang the radio.

"Ain't they supposed to be a Christmas tree?"

"Jesus," he said. "I forgot all about it." Throwing on a jacket and snatching a hatchet from beside the front door, he stomped out into the bright white morning.

By noon they were ready: the table set for eight, the kitchen bursting with food, the beribboned tree standing in the living room, the whole house redolent with turkey and spruce and burning wood. Then the Wares' old Nash and the

Grotes' Cadillac pulled into the yard, one behind the other. Greenleaf met them at the door and ushered them in, expansive and beaming.

"Merry Christmas, folks."

"Why, Alcott, you sure look peckish today. Merry Christmas to you."

"Merry Christmas, Maggie. You look like you're really starting to fill out there."

"And how are you, Evelyn? That's a nice-looking sweater you got on."

"Oh, Lin. Get along with you. *Everybody* gets this big. I expect I'll get a lot bigger than this, even."

"Alcott give it to me."

"How's things, Sheriff?"

"Say, dear, the customers still keep asking about you. Guess I'll have to tell them that you got yourself a little baby factory up here, and you're just getting ready to release your first model."

"Going good. Nobody's doing anything they shouldn't that I know about. Nice and quiet. I hear you're still changing a few tires for Frank Tuttle. You like it okay?"

"Goodness, Lin, don't say *that*. They'll think all I want to do is be pregnant."

"Ayuh."

"Ha, ha."

"Margaret, can Bessie and I help with anything in the kitchen?"

"Well, there ain't much left to do," said Margaret doubtfully.

At that instant came the roar of an unmuffled automobile turning off the road. "What's that?" asked Bessie Grote.

"It's Leslie," said Evelyn. "He's come."

"So he has," said Greenleaf.

There was a knock at the door. He opened it; outside stood a tall man in a pea jacket and blue jeans, about twenty-five, bare-headed with long dark hair slicked back. The man smiled loosely, his wide lips moist and gleaming in the crisp air. " 'Lo. Evelyn home?"

"Ayuh," he said. "Come in."

Evelyn came up to them. "This is Leslie Terror. This is my brother-in-law, Alcott."

"Yeah? Howdy do, Alcott. Actually, the name's Terrera. It's Wop."

"That so? Good to see you. Come on in. This is Sheriff and Mrs. Ware from Wiscasset, and these are the Grotes, from Bath. Say. Anybody feel like a Christmas beer?"

"Say, now, that'd be good," said Leslie, and the other men nodded. The women, except for Evelyn, were disappearing into the kitchen. Greenleaf followed them in, returning shortly with five cans of Schlitz, each of which in turn he clamped against his body and opened. He then began to distribute them.

"You a sheriff?" Leslie was asking Sheriff Ware. He was evidently suffering from a bad cold, for even as he spoke he snuffled hard, causing a drop of glistening opaque mucus hanging over his upper lip to dart back into his nostril like a frightened rabbit. Before the sheriff could reply to his question, he hawked loudly; there was a great crackle of phlegm breaking into his mouth. He stepped to the door, opened it, and spat out into the snow. "Jesus," he said, wiping his mouth on his sleeve. "I got this cold, and it's a scummy bastard."

"That time of year," said Greenleaf sympathetically.

"Sure is," agreed the sheriff. "I got a deputy, Ed Leeman. You might know him, Alcott." Greenleaf shook his head. "Well, every Christmas Ed's wife makes him go over to her parents for a big dinner. He hates it. Mrs. Bailey, his mother-in-law, is a pretty tough customer, and she rubs Ed kind of cross-grained. So, for the past week he's been going without wearing his socks trying to catch a cold so he wouldn't have to go." The men chuckled, and the sheriff continued. "But he just couldn't catch one. Stayed as healthy as a cricket. Then, yesterday morning before he come in to work, Mrs. Bailey called them up and told them she has a bad cold herself, and would they please stay home this Christmas. So Ed put his socks back on, happy as a pig in butter, and drove in to the office."

The sheriff paused. "Damned thing was that by three o'clock yesterday afternoon he got his cold. A real baster. He was coughing and sneezing so much that he had to go home to bed. Ha, ha."

The men all guffawed and gulped at their beers as if they were medicinal potions.

"Serves him right," said Evelyn suddenly.

They all turned to look at her, and the sudden attention made her flush. It was as if her words had broken her apart from the rest of them like a calving iceberg except that there was no actual motion; she seemed illuminated by a nearly visible aura, isolate, insular, beautiful. A moment of collective sexual epiphany: each of the men saw her as if for the first time—black curls tumbling to her shoulders, smooth white face and red glossy mouth, swelling pointed breasts underneath the white sweater, small waist and wide hips flaring beneath an old red skirt. As the men stared, she put up her hand to touch, almost defensively, the silver necklace she wore; her painted fingernails against the sweater became to the men drops of blood on a field of snow. They stood silent, confused, yet each acutely aware that they were all part of this moment, that they all shared this perception. She for her part tried to pretend that she did not understand what was happening, although she of course did. She had first seen the expression that covered each of their faces nearly five years earlier upon the face of Francis Nesbitt, her seventh-grade teacher; and she had doubtless seen it many times since. So she stood there, haughty and flushed, while the four men gazed upon her like an object—of wonder, of doom.

Finally, though, she broke the spell, snapping at one of them (who was in this respect no more guilty than any other): "Shut your mouth, Leslie."

Later, at the table, apparently overwhelmed by the dinner laid before them, Greenleaf, Lindall, and the sheriff sat quiet and subdued. Leslie, however, rose amiably to the occasion, entertaining the women with stories of life in Brunswick, told loudly through mouthfuls of mashed potatoes and turkey.

"I like Brunswick. When I got out of the Navy, I was stationed there, so I thought I'd stick around and get me a job. I'm from Worcester, Mass., actually. One time before I got my discharge, this buddy and me went into a bar, the State, for a couple of drinks. There was these three clam diggers in there, just stinking stiff, you know? just blind, and one of them turns and sees us. He screams out, 'Swabbies,' which is what they call sailors in Brunswick, and all of a sudden decks my buddy—just knocks him flat. So I threw the guy out on his butt—and his two pals too—and the owner comes up to me and says, 'Mister, if you ever want a job, you got one.' So now I tend that same bar."

"My stars and garters," said Emily Ware.

"Were they big fellows?" asked Margaret.

"The first guy wasn't so tall, but he was some wide, I'll tell you. Must have weighed in at over two hundred. And one of the others was bigger then me, and I ain't no featherweight."

"And you didn't have any trouble with them?" asked Bessie Grote.

"Naw. None to speak of."

"Well, it's a good thing all them fellows is up in Cumberland County," said the sheriff. "I'd hate to have to be the one who tells them where to go."

Everyone laughed. Leslie looked past Evelyn beside him to Greenleaf at the end of the table. "Say, Alcott. Evelyn tells me you're a mechanic. That right?"

"Ayuh."

"You any good?"

"So-so."

"I'm having some trouble with my Ford."

"That so?"

"Yeah. Runs a little ragged, especially when I'm pushing it up over seventy."

"Gracious," said Emily. "You don't drive that fast, I hope."

"He sure does," asserted Evelyn with quick pride blazing on her face.

"Well, bring it in," said Greenleaf. "Tuttle's Garage in Wiscasset. We'll take a look at it."

There was a pause. Then Leslie spoke again, his voice rising in innocent inquiry, "Do you have much trouble doing motor work?"

"How do you mean?"

"Well, you ain't got that hand."

The slight smile on Greenleaf's mouth glazed like porcelain and Evelyn stared down into her plate. The others—excepting only Leslie himself, who was obliviously finishing off a last piece of turkey—sensed immediately the tension, and gazed from one to the other as he answered: "Oh, just brute strength and ignorance."

"No, really. How can you turn in a screw, say?"

He took a breath and then spoke quickly, looking all the while at Evelyn, who continued to stare red faced at the remains of her dinner. "There are ways. I got some screw-drivers with screw clips to help hold the screws on till you get them started. Sometimes you can just do it one-handed, especially with a short screwdriver. Some other times you can use a blob of grease to kind of glue the screw to the driver. Just takes a little practice."

"Well, I'll be damned."

Greenleaf relaxed as suddenly as he had tensed, then became expansive: "You come down to the shop someday and I'll let you watch"; and the crisis was over. They passed on to other topics, and forgot it.

Only afterward, the dishes washed, the guests departed (the Wares and the Grotes had left first; Leslie had hung around a bit longer until Evelyn made it clear that she had no intention of going back to Brunswick with him), the house restored to normal, they sat around the wood stove, the three of them, and Evelyn asked, "Well, Alcott, what did you think about old Leslie?"

He thought an instant and grinned. "Him, sissy? Why—he is a terror, all right. Talks just like a shit salesman with his mouth full of samples."

There was a moment of silence, and then high and clear came Evelyn's shriek, joyous and unrestrained and shrill, breaking over them like shattering glass; Greenleaf sat there smiling; and at last, uncertainly, hesitantly, Margaret began also to laugh.

4

It had been a long winter, especially for Margaret. Now April was nearly upon them, yet snow still covered the ground and their unborn child still skulked within her womb. Her term seemed to her endless. At the end of each day she felt crushed by the fetal weight, drained by the osmotic absorption of her vitality. But even exhausted, she could not sleep. Nights she would lie awake alone (by mutual decision, Greenleaf had moved out into the living room shortly after Christmas, leaving her space to thrash about the bed in a vain search for some position of comfort), wishing desperately for her release, and growing more and more sure that she, like the Mrs. Greenleaf who had preceded her, would find it only in the soft chilly shroud of her grave. Although she never told her husband of her fears nor even reproached him for her discomfort, she began to give signs of her desperation by making an occasional uncharacteristic gesture. As she came to believe in the certainty of her parturient death, she grew strangely truculent and spoke once or twice in tones that were for her almost reckless.

One March evening at supper Greenleaf announced his intention to quit the job in Wiscasset after the baby was born. "I can get the used parts trade going again for the summer, and then I'll be right here if you need anything, Margaret."

"What about me?" demanded Evelyn.

"How's that, sissy?"

"How'm I going to get to work?"

"We'll see. Maybe we can get you a car."

"Huh? Of my own? You serious?"

"You're eighteen, ain't you? That ought to be old enough to have a car. I can try to fire up that old Pontiac my father got for me."

"You mean it?"

"We'll see about it."

Suddenly Margaret spoke in a voice strange to both of them: tired, flat, harsh, nonetheless deliberate and certain. "You know, Alcott, I had always counted on having that Pontiac for myself."

Evelyn flared. "Goddamnit, he said I could have it."

"I didn't know you wanted a car, Margaret."

"Well, I never had one before. Course, Evelyn can use it for work if she wants. But I want it."

"Ayuh. Well, now, that's what I meant. It'll be your car all right."

"Goddamnit—"

"Shut up, Evelyn," said Greenleaf quickly and firmly; and Margaret added, "That's right, Evelyn. The Pontiac is mine."

She angrily subsided, and they finished the rest of the meal—all of them—in vaguely astounded silence.

About a week later, at four thirty on the afternoon of Friday, March 31, Greenleaf and Evelyn together in the pickup pulled into the yard, home from work. Evelyn was laughing so shrilly about something as they walked into the house that at first they did not hear Margaret calling weakly from the bedroom: "Alcott! Alcott!"

"Ayuh. We're here." He rushed across the room.

"I been having some pains."

"Well, then, I guess it's really going to come out of there. When did they start?"

"About noon."

"Jesus. You could have called me at work."

"I thought I wouldn't bother you."

"Jesus. Well, I suppose I better go and get Mary. Evelyn, you stay here and look after your sister." And he was gone in a blur, banging and sliding the truck up the road toward North Whitefield. When he came to the path to Mary's cabin, he slammed on the brakes, locking the wheels on the ice: the truck slid majestically past the path and turned as it skidded, stopping at last fifty yards beyond and facing back in the direction from which it had come. He pulled up to the path and then was out and hurrying over the beaten snow to the cabin, rapping on the rough planks of the door and calling hoarsely: "Hey! Mary!"

The brown face peered out, black eyes brightening with recognition. "Aha. G'eenleaf. You baby come?"

"Seems to be knocking at the door. Can you come now?"

"Aha. Bien. I get my bag, eh? Kii."

"Ayuh."

Then they were speeding back over that same icy frost-heaved road, the truck roaring and rattling as before, the old woman smiling with delight and bouncing on the seat beside him as fragile and as brittle as an egg. He was almost surprised to see that she was still intact when they arrived at the house.

Inside they found Margaret lying in her bed, white-faced, sweating. Evelyn, who was sitting beside her, looked up in astonishment as Mary followed Greenleaf into the bedroom. "Who's that?"

"Mary Newell," he replied. "She's the midwife."

Evelyn's eyes were wide. "She's a Indian, ain't she? Or a nigger. What's she know about being a midwife?"

"She delivered me."

She stalked out of the room. Mary, who had paused in the doorway all the while smiling as if she had not understood a word Evelyn had said, stepped aside for her and then came inside. She set her bag on a table beside the bed under the window, pulled out several objects wrapped in white linen, and arrayed them before her. "Need hot water and clean towel. Many towel." As he went into the kitchen, she smiled down at Margaret. "Baby come, hah?"

She nodded weakly. "I guess so." Suddenly she gasped. "Huh. There it is."

"How often hurt?"

"Pains come about every half hour or so. Maybe less."

"When start?"

"Around noon."

"Aha."

Greenleaf entered. "Here's the towels."

"Là," she said, pointing. "Hot water?"

"Coming."

"Bien. You make coffee, eh? Ver' strong, with sugar. I wash hands. It be plenty time yet."

She was right. Margaret's labor ran steady and slow all that evening and on into the night. She lay on her side under a sheet while the old woman sat beside her, wiping her forehead. Greenleaf watched as they seemed to grow together, to merge—the one old and brown and small, the other younger and white and bloated with child—crossing the barriers of race, age, and culture to the simple basis of their common sex and the pain unique to it. The midwife appeared to subsume some part of this pain and thus become almost as much of a participant in the birth as the mother or the fetus. When the labor began at last to intensify and quicken, Mary gave her a worn piece of oak that was vaguely the size and shape of a phallus, saying, "Here. Hold this. Squeeze them pains inside this wood."

As Margaret took the stick, the midwife helped her roll onto her back. Bent brown fingers pulled down the sheet that covered her and laid some of the towels on the bed between her legs. There she lay, nightdress raised to her breasts, knees drawn up and spread apart, stomach large and veined and distended, vulva slightly open and vulnerable beneath the tangled hair of her pubis. Mary turned to Greenleaf. "You stay?"

He nodded. Just then Margaret gasped; clear liquid spurted from her vagina almost as if it had been spit from it, falling onto the towels. Piss? he thought, but Mary said, "Bien. Water come. Baby ready to show up next."

Still for another half-hour or so, although Margaret groaned and strained and squeezed the piece of oak, he could see no further change. Once Evelyn peered angrily inside the room, but just for an instant, and so absorbed were the others that they scarcely noticed her. Greenleaf stood unblinking at the foot of the bed, watching the two, filled with emotions he did not describe to himself except in noting with surprise that what he considered love was not among them—leaving fear and awe and pity and, probably as well, disgust. Too, the knowledge that on an evening more than twenty-three years ago this same scene had been played in this same room with this same midwife and he had been the result of that scene further sobered him. So he stood silently by, gazing into his wife's vagina, which rhythmically opened and closed in vacuolar frenzy, until at last he saw there a shiny white circle, dime sized, like a blind eye staring emptily out at him. From her position kneeling beside Margaret's knees, Mary could see it also; and she turned a gap-toothed grin toward Greenleaf. "Head. Good, eh? Not breech."

And slowly, constantly, the dime became a nickel, then a quarter, a half dollar, advancing, receding, advancing a bit more. The skin, he saw, was very pale and shiny, and was streaked with fine black hairs plastered down wetly. Mary placed her hands gently beneath as much of the head as protruded, feeling for its progress. Margaret groaned and bore down. The partial head was strained, then relaxed, then strained again, but seemed now to make no new advance. Mary grunted and spread wider the vulva, her fingers burrowing between the head and the vaginal tissue. Quickly they were withdrawn to snatch a pair of surgical scissors from the table; next one hand again dived alongside the infant head, the scissors following them, and then the outside thumb and forefinger, silver ringed, separated and conjoined with a snip: in horror Greenleaf watched blood (his wife's? his child's?) spurt from around her hands; "What?" he said in strangled tones, while Mary, reaching with one hand for two clamps from the table, with the other pulled past the now rapidly emerging head the umbilical cord—a slimy, blue-veined snake with a bleeding stump where its head might have been—and clamped it. Then the neck was free, and he saw that the clamped cord was still wrapped once around it. She reached in again and somehow extracted the other end of the cord, which she likewise clamped. By this time bloody infant shoulders were emerging, Margaret all the while groaning and pressing, then the waist, the child curling upward toward the mother until its hips passed the vulva, when it fell back into Mary's hands. At that instant he saw its tiny penis and realized he had now a son: pale white, almost blue, shiny, and still. "Is it alive?" he asked, and Mary lifted him by the feet and with one soft, wrinkled, blood-wet hand slapped the glistening buttocks. The infant gasped—a thin, short gurgle—and began irregular respiration. Mary looked up at him with her bright black eyes. "Aha. You have a boy." He could scarcely hear her for the roaring in his ears.

Later, the umbilical cord tied and trimmed, the child washed and swaddled, the placenta expelled, the bedding changed, Mary boiled some yellow ash leaves in a pan on the stove. She brought the steaming tea in to Margaret. "Here. Drink this. Make you clean and strong again."

"Ugh," said Margaret, swallowing. Then remembering something else, she called to her husband. "Alcott. What time was he born?"

"About two o'clock."

"So it's April Fools' Day. April Fool. Ain't he something."

"Ayuh."

That afternoon he realized it was the first day of a new month. For the first time in many years he had not begun it with his father's "Rabbit-rabbit," and his happiness at his son's birth seemed slightly diminished by the omission. Margaret, on the other hand, was radiant with joy, for she had been granted not only a son but her life as well. She never spoke of her earlier premonitions of death, putting them completely out of her mind; instead she talked of the future, with rich words of happiness and hope.

5

THE infant lay on his back in the crib, motionless. His eyes were pale blue and lusterless, looking up at the ceiling. April sunshine, breaking through the window beside him, illuminated tiny specks of dust afloat in the air. Calm, peace: at the center of the vortex, the eye of the hurricane, here, all quiet and serene.

Now something was beside him: a shape, a scent, a sound, all of which he could at least perceive. He squalled briefly, then subsided. It was not a sound of communication exactly, but of community—a noise lying at the root of language, but not yet language itself: the salutation of infants and imbeciles.

"What's a matter, baby? You still hungry?" He was

picked up, his head supported by a hand; suddenly a nipple was thrust against his mouth. He sucked for a bit but soon stopped, either losing interest in—or altogether forgetting—what he was doing. Then he was laid against something and patted on his back until a bubble wrapped in milk rolled up his throat and splashed out of his mouth.

Sounds impinged, from elsewhere. He was put back into the crib, covered with a blanket. He resumed his misty gaze at the ceiling as the Jovian voices boomed louder.

"Well, good Lord. Let's have a look at the little fellow."

"He's in here, Sheriff."

"Now, Bee, you be careful. You'll scare him."

"Well, there. Look at him. Cute as an ant's ear. Ain't much bigger than one either."

"Course he isn't. Why he's only—what is he now, Margaret, three weeks?"

"Uh, he was three weeks yesterday."

"Ha, ha."

The infant screwed up his face and began to cry.

"There. You've done it now, Bee. Oh, now, there. There."

The infant quieted.

"How'd you come to name him, Margaret? We was real surprised."

"Me, too. I was thinking of calling him after you and Lin Grote, Sheriff, because of all you two did for us. Bartholomew Lindall Greenleaf. But Alcott wouldn't say anything about that, one way or the other."

"It wouldn't have been an easy name to live with. 'Bartholomew' all by itself is no picnic, I can tell you."

"So he sat in front of the stove looking at that nasty leg of his dead father for hours and hours. I was ready to go ahead and name him myself, without asking. But finally he comes into the bedroom, looks at the baby, and says, 'Eustis.' That was all, but I could tell he meant it, so I didn't say anything. Just nodded."

All this was so much vibrating air to the infant, who, now that the threat of the loud sounder had been removed, lay still, still looking up. He might have been staring into the sun. Then the big voices left him in peace, were gone, and he did not remember they had come. No past, no future, only the fragile now, in the same way that only the here existed for him, and even that was ill perceived, vague and blurry. He lay there without motion except to breathe lightly and to blink, just looking at some indefinite point over his head, with pale blue eyes as blank and emotionless as a winter sky.

Guam

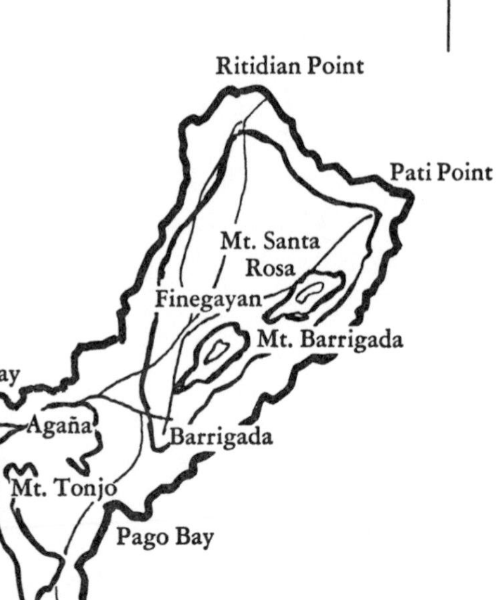

Scale: 1 inch = 6 miles

Contour interval: 300 feet

Map from *Guam: Operations of the 77th Division,* War Department (Washington, D.C.: 1946), p. 137.

V Guam

AN island in the South Pacific fifteen hundred miles east of the Philippines and sixteen hundred miles south of Japan, slipper-shaped with low mountains, the southernmost and largest member of a crescent archipelago (called for now the Marianas) that comprises also Rota, Tinian, Saipan, and others; an island finally bewildered by aggression as it lay on 10 August, 1944, bombed and broken and gouged from twenty-one days of American assault, three weeks during which nearly 55,000 American troops killed or captured 18,500 Japanese; an island which had seen better days:

as on 11 December, 1941, when 5,000 of the aforementioned suns of Nippon rose from Saipan and swarmed like cruel beetles over the island, easily overpowering the 419 Americans and some 20,000 native Chamorros, imprisoning most of the former and beheading some of the latter;

as on 20 June, 1898, when Captain Henry Glass, USN, sailed the U.S.S. *Charleston* into Agaña Bay and captured the island without bloodshed (the Spanish governor was unaware of his country's war with the United States and, mistaking the *Charleston*'s booming cannons for a salute, greeted her hospitably);

as on 6 March, 1521, when Fernando Magallanes landed at Umatac Bay and claimed the island together with the rest of the archipelago for Spain and for Carlos V, naming them *Los*

Ladrones, The Robbers, since some light-fingered Chamorro swam out one night and stole a boat (Magellan, seeing no humor in the occurrence, decided to teach the natives a lesson by killing seven of them and burning fifty of their houses);

as on that unrecorded date perhaps two millennia before Christ when the Chamorros themselves arrived, proto-Malayans from Asia, probably via the Carolines, and began setting up their complex society of warrior priests and formalized ritual war, where the loss of two men was sufficient to determine the victor of a battle;

and as on that day or year or whatever unit of time measures acts of creation, when the skin of the young planet heaved and folded and burst, throwing island and archipelago above the surface of the ocean until such time as men should at last discover strength enough to throw them entirely back.

1

ABOARD the transport the men's low voices wove a tapestry of complaints in the smoky air:

"Well, I wish to Christ we'd get off this fucking boat."

"What did the corporal tell you, Weinstein?"

"What's the matter, Wilson? Can't wait to be a hero?"

"I hear it's the Navy's fault. Them and their submarine alerts."

"I'll tell you one thing. That bastard won't last two days of combat."

"Ah, cram it."

"The runs, by God, they can be lethal. I know a guy who almost shit himself inside out on Kwajalein."

"Come on, Weinstein, what did he say?"

"By Jesus, Perrone, when I get home, I'll kill the bitch. I'll kill her."

"While we were in Eniwetok, I was watching him. He's a son of a bitch and a coward."

"He said that when it was time for us to land, we would be the first to know."

"Yeah, well, he told me to tell it to the Marines. The Marines? Fuck them. Fuck him, for that matter."

"What time is it, Greenleaf?"

"Wise-assed son of a bitch, ain't he?"

"About 2310."

"What'd he say?"

"Jesus Christ, it's past my bedtime. How long are we going to sit in this hole, anyway?"

Driven fifteen miles out to sea by a submarine scare, the transport had just steamed indignantly back to her launching area nearly three miles off Agat Beach. The men it transported—members of the Third Battalion, 305 Regimental Combat Team, Seventy-seventh Division, under the command of Major General Andrew D. Bruce, USA—now awaited the return of landing craft that had already carried the First and Second battalions ashore, as well as the First Provisional Marine Brigade, landing craft that should have also carried them ashore hours earlier to participate in this, W Day for Guam, 21 July, 1944.

Alcott Greenleaf was among them. A soldier on his seventeenth birthday and a PFC four months later, he had convinced a recruiting sergeant to accept him despite his obvious youth (he was five feet seven inches tall, and his voice had not yet deepened) by challenging him to an arm-wrestling contest. The sergeant, though not himself a large man, laughed at such presumption and immediately set his right elbow on the table between them, arm upraised. Greenleaf met his hand and pulled it toward him until his elbow touched the table too; then he squeezed the other's hand suddenly, not pushing down but merely resisting the opposing push and continuing to squeeze. Beads of sweat popped from the sergeant's face. "Hey," he said, but nothing more; and for fourteen minutes both sat at the table silently, not moving the locked hands more than an inch either way, until the sergeant finally grunted, "Goddamnit. Okay." Still, it took him nearly forty minutes to fill out Greenleaf's papers, his hand trembled so.

"All right, men, off your asses. Company A, let's go!" Picking up packs and rifles, they moved quickly to the deck where they could hear more clearly the distant mortar shells exploding, then down the gangway by platoons to LCM's bobbing in dark waters. Aboard the craft Greenleaf could see the stars and the shoreline and vague forms beside him, could smell the moist mixture of salt air and sweat, could hear the sound of the men near him talking, water splashing, and the LCM's motor idling as they circled and waited.

"What do you think, Weinstein? Is this going to be cake?"

"You got a cigarette?"

"Well, I'm glad we're going in behind the Marines."

"I just wish I had some kaopectate."

"You bet, buddy."

"That sounds like you, Weinstein. I swear to Christ."

"What I don't understand is how come it's so goddamned late at night. Somebody must have really fucked up."

"Oh, stuff it, Wilson."

"Christ, we're still circling. When are we going to head in?"

"All right, men, button it up. We're going in now and expect to hit the reef around 0230 hours. The word is that there are no LVT's once we get to the reef, so you're going to have to wade the rest of the way in. There's a channel to the shore about waist-deep, and it's low tide right about now, so you shouldn't have near as much trouble as the First Battalion did. Enemy fire on the beach is described as very light, and under darkness you won't be as exposed as you would in daylight. We will establish a position in the northern sector of Beach Red and dig in. Try to stay with the unit. If you get separated, find the red zone as soon as you can. Our objective is support only and we do not anticipate any direct enemy engagement at this time. That's it. As you were."

"Christ, I told you. It's a piece of cake. Like pouring piss out of a boot."

"Jesus. Two thirty in the morning? This is going to be hell on my complexion. I need my beauty sleep."

"Goddamnit, I got to go to the can."

"You need more than sleep, Walker. You need plastic surgery."

"You'll have to go over the side, Perrone. Be careful. Don't fall in."

"What do you think, Greenleaf? A piece of cake, right?"

"Watch it, Perrone. You'll give the Japs a target they can't miss."

"Me, Wilson? I think you are going to eat them Japs right up."

"Holy God. Poison gas. Where's my mask?"

"Christ, Perrone. What did you eat, anyhow?"

"Aw kiss it, you guys."

"Not on your goddamned life."

Twenty-two soldiers rode in the LCM. They carried both blessings and equipment from their nation, American prayers plus a hardware store each: steel helmet, gas mask, life belt, rifle, bayonet, ammunition bandoleers, grenades, wire cutters, two canteens, first-aid kit, machete, and light pack. Most of them thought it was sufficient, but they did so without basis. All save three—two corporals and a sergeant—were green, had never shot at a uniform worn by a man shooting back, and thus had never had occasion to question the necessity of what they carried. If anything, they thought it was too much.

In silence now they endured the wait in their several ways. Greenleaf forced himself blank and leaned against the gunwale, caressed by rushing air, lulled by the throbbing engine of the LCM. A private named Bernard Weinstein from Brooklyn mentally compared his abilities with those of his platoon leader and judged himself (and not for the first time either) far superior. Another private, Jack Walker from Chicago, handled his machete and dreamed he stood at some Loop bar with whores hanging from each arm like diamonds. Private Sammy Perrone of Boston clamped his buttocks tight against his loosened bowels, fearful even to fart. And next to Greenleaf, Private Gerald X. Wilson, West Hartford, recited to himself without moving his lips an Ave and a Pater Noster for every finger on each hand.

Finally, with a dull ferocious scrape the landing craft bottomed on rock. Wilson spoke at once, softly, desperately: "Greenleaf. I can't swim. I hate the fucking water."

"All right, men, this is the reef. You wade or swim from here. Everybody got their water wings? You can see the shore by the starlight. Try to stick together. Over the side."

"Greenleaf."

"Ayuh. I heard you. Look, it ain't deep. You can—"

"I'll slip. I know. Help me."

"Christ."

"Greenleaf."

"Christ. All right. Jump off beside me. Grab onto my rifle butt."

He sat on the deck of the LCM, his legs over the side, one

hand against the deck, the other holding the barrel of the M-1, which linked him with Wilson—terrible, temporary Siamese twins. "Now!" and he pushed: falling out from the craft, then snapped back at the shoulder, finally whipping after him the reluctant Wilson like a huge Yo-Yo. Greenleaf stood waist deep in the dark, tepid water and the other man scrabbled up his back, coughing and spluttering, almost pushing him over.

"Relax, Wilson, for Christ's sake."

"Yeah. Shit fire."

They stepped tentatively along the channel in the dark, Agat Beach a pale crescent nearly a mile away. Vague shadowed forms bobbed ahead of them. Occasionally an exploding mortar broke over the sounds of the men calling to one another.

"How you doing, Perrone?"

"Did you dub up your boots? Inspection when we get ashore."

"Don't get too close behind me, Walker. I'll blow you right out of the water."

"Hey, Greenleaf. This is a fucking piece of cake," said Wilson not loudly and fell without warning into an underwater mortar crater. Greenleaf was pulled off balance and dragged down. Struggling back to his feet, he yanked the rifle toward him; Wilson came up, gasping and choking.

"Goddamnit, Wilson. You are worse than my Christless father, and he's a cripple. Now you listen. You step careful. And if you say one more word, I'll let go of this goddamned rifle and let you drown."

The water was warm and thick, like blood.

Without words they waded along the channel, its depth ranging from waist to neck. Once they came to a break in it, a hiatus five yards wide, perhaps blown out by mines or mortars. Wilson stood in water to his belt while Greenleaf swam with his rifle to the other side.

"You got to swim across, Wilson."

"I can't. Help me."

"Hold your hands out in front of you and jump toward me. Kick with your feet. When you feel the rifle butt, muckle right on to it."

There was no answer.

"Come on, Wilson."

"Look. I got a ring my mother gave me, I'll give you. Real gold. With a diamond. Honest to God. Please. Help me."

"I am. Jump toward me, Wilson. Come on."

"No. Help me."

"Goddamnit." Greenleaf's voice was low and vicious. "You dirty, lousy, yellow shit, Wilson. You goddamned chicken-shit. Your mother! Fuck her. Your mother must have yellow all over her belly, just like a shitless Jap, you suck-faced weasel. You—"

"Bastard!" screamed Wilson. "You shut up about my mother!" and leaped across the void toward the voice of ice, flailing and kicking desperately. Greenleaf thrust the rifle butt beneath the splashing, felt a hand strike and grasp it, and pulled him to shallow water. When he stood erect, Greenleaf said nothing more but wheeled toward the shore. Soon the water lapped at their knees. Wilson dropped the rifle butt; then they were on the beach.

Greenleaf walked quickly without looking back to the first group of men he saw. "You guys know where the A Company bivouac is? Beach Red?"

"Able? Shit, fellow, I don't know. Any you guys?"

"Try up the beach there."

"We're looking for the rest of Charlie. I'd like to know who's running this frigging party. What a fuck-up."

"You know what time it is?"

A mortar exploded inland. It sounded softer and more distant here than the explosions they had heard from the water. Greenleaf looked at his watch, its luminescence shining like a star on his wrist.

"Ayuh. It's 0335 hours."

"Thanks. Take care, now."

"Ayuh. You too, Charlie."

He marched up the beach, his fatigues clinging to his body, sticky and sodden, the pack straps cutting into his shoulders. His back and crotch itched with salt. Mosquitoes buzzed by his ears, tiny bombers. From behind him Wilson spoke: "Hey."

He continued to walk.

"Greenleaf. You listen."

"Shut up."

"You say one more thing about my mother, I'll kill you."

"Goddamnit, shut up."

When they found Company A just before dawn, Greenleaf sat down by the red light gathering in the sky and carefully cleaned his rifle.

2

THE assault on Guam consisted of two beachheads, one north of the Orote Peninsula on Agaña Bay conducted by the Third Marine Division, and the other south of Orote on Agat Bay spearheaded by the First Provisional Marine Brigade and supported by the Army's Seventy-seventh Division. While the Third Marine pushed down the coast toward Apra Harbor, the brigade drove north to the neck of Orote and then onto the peninsula itself where the island's primary airstrip lay glittering like a jewel. The Seventy-seventh filled in behind them to bridge the gap between beachheads, capturing easily Mount Tenjo, one of the little volcanic bumps that on Guam pass for mountains. Although the Seventy-seventh met little resistance, the Third Marine experienced severe Japanese opposition as it struggled south to link the beachheads. On 27 July, however, the enemy forces suddenly dissolved in front of the Marine advance, which was left fighting air, blessed miracle. It became apparent that the Japanese who could were retiring to the northern half of the island presumably to stage a counteroffensive there. Meanwhile, the brigade encountered the bitterest fighting of the entire assault on the Orote Peninsula, where enemy troops, their backs against the edge of the sea and unable to retreat, had determined not to die cheaply. Finally, though, on 28 July the assault was over: the peninsula had been cleared of all enemy troops and the final beachline stretched firm and intact from Agaña to Agat.

The newly liberated territory lay quivering in the sun like a worried bone, as if chewed by the teeth of a dragon. On the reef hung several broken landing craft; pits and ruts from weapons and machinery scarred the beach. Inland the *lemonchina*—waist-high, long-thorned brush covering much of the island—oozed sap where it had been bent down and crushed. Great clods of soil had everywhere been wrenched from the ground, and the broken land gaped in astonishment. Each day just before noon the rains came for an hour to wash clean these wounds of the earth, commingling its dust with the blood and sweat of dead soldiers and also of those who survived.

Of the 5,987 (mostly Marine) casualties in the assault, 958 were deaths. These had been collected, and other men now walked where they had lain. Thirty-seven men in Greenleaf's company had been hurt, but no one in his platoon was among them.

At first, after the initial landing had been accomplished, Company A was assigned the supply dumps, hauling and bucking tons of matériel over marshy, muddy ground. Greenleaf hated it, was maddened by it—the hot, stinking swamps, the sweat, the sudden rains that soaked but never cooled him, the furious mosquitoes, and the omnivorous, unyielding mud. Several times, jacking up a Jeep, say, and mired in the miasmal muck, he would all at once see his father lying on the couch in the front room, the clumsy prosthetic leg removed and tossed onto the floor. Perhaps the old man would be drinking beer in the cool summer breeze. Such a vision would seize Greenleaf, fill him with white fury, swamp him, fling him awash. He could not wait until he got into combat, got killed, something, he did not know.

These rages deserted him as quickly as they came on, leaving behind only a slight bitter taste on his tongue and a momentary loss of strength. Because the one visible symptom he displayed was a short paralysis, something like a petit mal seizure, the other men never noticed them. Only Wilson was even aware of his capacity for fury, and he mentioned it to no one, not even to Greenleaf himself, for the two men had not spoken since the landing.

The supply dump detail lasted two days. When on 24 July Company A was relieved by the supply battalion, the men were overjoyed; combat and even death seemed preferable to their present Sisyphean assignment. The company then moved inland due east about two miles from the beach over the broken terrain and there established a base not far from the attack line. Before its platoons could be deployed on patrols, however, the company commander received orders to link up with companies C and D and move northeast toward Mount Tenjo. Up to this time nobody in Company A had fired a weapon and the only casualty since the landing was a private who had broken his foot when he dropped a case of K rations on it. "Christ, that shit will kill you even if you *don't* eat it," said Jack Walker, and they all laughed.

The ground over which they traveled was high and sparse, a six-mile ridge running from Mount Lamlam north to North Tenjo. Here the *lemonchina* had given way to swordgrass and the terrain was firm—yet the men were not comfortable. They marched nervously, occasionally looking over their right shoulders, half expecting hoards of Japanese banzai troops to rise up at their flank. To the north they could hear remote explosions of the war, but their vicinity was silent and empty.

"Where the hell are they?" muttered Perrone, almost to himself; and Weinstein, ahead of him, answered, "They're up north. Hear them? This area has been cleaned out."

"Oh, yeah?"

At his words a Browning automatic rifle had begun chattering somewhere ahead of them, but another voice spoke up: "Can it. That's us."

At about 1200 hours on 25 July the three companies established positions along the ridge a mile or so south of Mount Tenjo. From these points they proposed to send reconnaissance patrols east to determine the enemy's concentrations and at the same time to create some offensive thrusts to keep him off-balance.

Part of Greenleaf's platoon was one of the five patrols sent out on the morning of 26 July. The eastern slope of the ridge was sprayed thoroughly with Brownings and the company's antitank gun; and when no enemy response was detected, the five groups of men moved down slowly, cautiously, toward the lower jungle and the distant sea, fanning apart so that one patrol would not become a target for another.

The men traveled in a line, two abreast. There were ten in

the patrol with the scout, a corporal named Crocker reassigned to them from the First Battalion, at the head beside the platoon leader, Second Lieutenant Barton. Greenleaf walked near the end beside Perrone.

As they descended, the shrubs thickened and rose higher until they were firmly closed in the jungle: weeds, trailing vines, strand trees, lianas, and again the ubiquitous *lemon-china.* Forced to hack a path, by twos they took turns standing at the head of the line and swinging their machetes for two minutes at the tenacious growth. Fifteen minutes and nearly four hundred yards later, bending down to chop free a vine, Greenleaf heard a whine, a smack, the sharp bark of a rifle; as he dropped to the ground, he looked up to see Perrone stumble back, eyes wide with confusion and fear, blood pouring from a sudden hole in his neck; saw behind this the others cave and collapse to the sides of the trail and into the jungle; and then turned his head to the growth in front of him, straining to see the invisible target, the hidden assassin. Dropping his machete, he crawled to the left into the brush as the men behind him began firing blindly into the trees.

He knew what he was doing, knew that at the other end of the line defined at that instant by a point six inches above his head and Perrone's throat was the end of the enemy rifle barrel, and thus knew more or less where the sniper sat peering at leaves for more flashes of movement. He crawled through the undergrowth, stabbed and clawed by branches and thorns, what noise he was making generally concealed by the rattling fire of the men behind him. In a sense he was not thinking anything as he wormed along; long ago in another avatar he had stalked another game in another forest, had killed his first deer (a seven-point buck, which was not at all a bad initiation) at the age of nine in the woods behind his father's house. Here and now he moved with a measure of the same unconscious stealth and grace he had always hunted with. To his right overhead a rifle banged. He at once lay still but, hearing no whine, realized he was not the sniper's target. At the same time he smelled a faint strange rankness—almost like skunk cabbage—which he had not before noticed in the jungle. He crawled toward the sound of the shot, his nostrils flaring in response to the increasing odor.

Then he saw leaves trembling in a tree ten feet away. He moved slightly, saw the sniper's head, aimed with grave deliberation, and gently squeezed off. There was an instant of startled silence following the shot, and then the body, bones and blood, crashed from the tree and hit the ground like a sack of meal.

The patrol was about twenty yards away. After a moment of silence he called to them. He stood up as Second Lieutenant Barton led them cautiously out of the jungle toward him. "Nice work, Greenleaf."

"Ayuh. Thanks."

The lieutenant went over to the dead sniper, who had been shot through the neck. "Phew. Smell that. Like hot piss."

Some of the men laughed, and the patrol was resumed. It encountered no further enemy activity although it covered nearly four miles, and Greenleaf hummed to himself quietly for most of the rest of the mission.

The next day companies A and C drove north the rest of the way to Mount Tenjo, leaving D Company to hold the position already secured. They met little resistance, military or topographical, as they swept up to the tiny mountain and that evening were comfortably situated just east of its thousand-foot peak. For the next three days, while the Third Marine Division was struggling to unite the northern beachhead with the southern, the two companies maintained their positions along the attack line. During this period they suffered no casualties.

On the morning of 29 July, Second Lieutenant Barton briefed his platoon: "Men, I want to bring you all up to date on the whole picture. In case you've lost count, we've been here nine days. The assault of the island is as of today complete. Link-up has been made with the Marines. At 0900 hours this morning the attack line was declared intact. The Marines on Orote report the capture of the airfield. All they have left to do is mop up the peninsula. Enemy kill is estimated at four thousand."

"Well, all right now."

"Shit fire."

"Send in the Marines. Them bastards. They do good work."

"Aw, them pricks. Frig them all. They give me a pain in the ass, if you want to know."

"So now we began the pursuit phase of this operation. The brass thinks that the Japs have been retreating to the northern half of the island and are getting together some welcoming parties for us up there. We've split the north in half—the Seventy-seventh gets the eastern sector and the Third Marines will take the west.

"Tomorrow we're due to be relieved by the Marine Brigade, which will assume our present positions. The entire Third Battalion will consolidate and move into position for the jump-off, which is set for 0630 hours, the day after tomorrow. For today, we maintain the attack line, just like we have been. Any questions?"

There were none. "Okay, men, as you were."

"By Jesus, Wilson, this one's going to be the bitch."

"Hey. Where's Crocker?"

"What do you mean, boy?"

"I don't know. How should I know, for Christ's sake? He's probably off someplace taking a dump."

"Well, we'll be walking right down their throats. They'll be sitting up there with their backs against the wall just waiting for us. Like the Marines on Orote. A fucking bitch, and you better believe it."

"He told me this joke. You know how come fall is like the Japanese Air Force?"

"You may be right, Weinstein."

"Fall? No. How come, wise guy?"

"What do you say, Greenleaf?"

"Because there's always a little Nip in the air."

"About what?"

"Haw. What a card."

"About the move north. Weinstein says it's going to be a bitch."

"Nip in the air. Honest to Christ, Walker. I don't know about you."

"Haw."

"I don't say nothing about it at all."

3

AT the waist of the island sat Agaña, a sort of omphalic nexus from which radiated three dirt roads: one west and then south along the coast to Agat, a second southeast toward Pago Bay and then south, the third northeast to Finegayan and points north. This last forked, a few hundred yards from its origin. The fork ran due east for five miles where it was met by another route coming south from Finegayan, thus creating a right triangle of roads, the vertices lying at Agaña, Finegayan, and a tiny village of less than fifteen buildings named Barrigada.

A valuable prize for invading armies, this Barrigada, a treasure despite its inconsequential size: possessing a reservoir and pumping station, it was the primary waterhole for the riverless northeastern sector of the island.

Company A of the Third Battalion was positioned a half mile east of the village on the afternoon of 2 August. Greenleaf's platoon had been halted in a clearing of swordgrass just north of the Agaña–Barrigada road. The men gathered in knots, smoking, muttering among themselves.

"Well, I think we've been goddamned lucky."

"I just killed a mosquito as big as a fucking robin redbreast, I swear to Christ."

"Yeah, right, Weinstein. Well, you just count your blessings."

"Quick, Henry, the Flit."

"You heard what the lieutenant said, Weinstein. When them tanks get here, we go in and give them support. That's how lucky we are. Bravo Company went into that pisshole town this morning and cleaned it out, but they got the shit kicked out of them doing it. And the Japs are *still* sitting in the woods northeast of it."

"The Flit. I guess to hell the Flit. They ought to bomb the whole goddamned island with the Flit."

"Hey. Look at that. The boy has a Browning."

"Yeah, but Bravo didn't have any tanks."

"Christ, Greenleaf, a BAR. It's beautiful. Where'd you get it?"

"Honest to shit, Weinstein. You're as fucked up as a whore in church. The tanks don't protect us. We protect the tanks."

"I tell you, Weinstein. You stick close to Greenleaf and forget them damn tanks. That Browning there is worth three tanks any day of the week."

"Ayuh. The lieutenant give it to me."

"Thanks a lot, Crocker."

"All right, Sergeant, let's get these men up and moving."

"Right. Let's go, men."

In twenty minutes they were crouching at the edge of the jungle, looking across a wide field at the village. A hundred yards to their right the Agaña road unrolled sleepily toward the junction, which was hidden from their view by several buildings and surrounding trees. Four hundred yards in front of them was the Finegayan road; on the other side of it, close to the opposing jungle, sat a green tin-roofed shack. Beyond their cover nothing moved, nor could they hear a sound. The men huddled like actors in the wings before a play, the amphitheater outside lacking only an audience: as if that which conferred reality upon whatever they were about to perform was not the presence of live ammunition nor unbated bayonets nor even the promise of death, but simply the absence of someone who would watch them to applaud their successes and bemoan their failures, and who would thus transmute their ridiculous agony into the pure clean sublimity of art.

"Maybe they pulled back."

"Yeah. And maybe they grew feathers and flew to heaven."

And then with a shout Lieutenant Barton was out in front of them and they heard the faint but increasing rumble of the tanks, shattering the profound silence as they thundered along the road from Agaña, strewing clouds of dust in their wake. And the men broke from their cover and rushed low, like wind, through the knee-high swordgrass straight across the field toward that green shack, which sat like an emerald against the green velvet jungle beyond. Immediately the jungle began crackling and chattering at them, so they dropped and fired back at it while the four tanks roared triumphantly into the open, a haughty armada a hundred yards to their right, slowing now as they approached the town to reconnoiter the area. The men in the field and the jungle continued firing on each other.

Because of a slight swell in the field, Greenleaf and the others had yet some protection from enemy fire. He lay on his stomach, still two hundred yards from the road, spraying the jungle with the Browning, furiously, hopelessly. Then he stopped. A soldier darted by him and threw himself on the ground beside Lieutenant Barton, a yard away.

"Sir. Orders from Captain Condit, Able Company. You and your men are to follow the tanks through the town."

"Right. Sure. Through town. What the hell do they mean? The tanks are practically through the town right now. Look at them. Goddamnit."

The tanks were moving cautiously toward the first buildings, their cannons lashing out at them and the jungle beyond.

"We'll never get over there in time. Christ almighty. I just talked to a goddamned *colonel,* for Christ's sake, and if he doesn't know what the hell is going on, who does?"

"I don't know, Lieutenant."

He shouted down the line. "All right, men. We meet the tanks when they turn north on the Finegayan road. They won't have any trouble in the town. So we rush straight ahead to the road and that green shack. We pick up the tanks there.

"Oh, and Greenleaf."

"Ayuh?"

"Keep firing that goddamned rifle."

"Ayuh."

So they were running again, firing ahead at no visible targets, pumping lead into the jungle like water into a drain, hearing the enemy bullets burn by like terrible bees, stumbling over shell holes toward the road, a hundred yards, fifty, twenty, and finally diving into the shallow safety of the ditch, most of them anyway: back in the field lay a corporal named Louis Murcer with a shattered knee, a private named Lon Nettles with a bullet in his thigh, and almost at the ditch Jack Walker with a gaping hole in the center of his chest. Eighteen of twenty-one. From the ditch they fired into the jungle, a soft yielding amorphous sponge that could absorb whatever they shot into it, even spit some back. Greenleaf whimpered in fury and wrapped his finger tight around the trigger of the Browning.

Now, glory to God, came the tanks! already through the town, churning obliquely from the road toward the jungle, cannons thundering blindly into the green growth. The lieutenant shouted, "The shack! The shack!" and the men charged out of the ditch and across the road, adding their rounds to those of the tanks, directing great and lethal cascades of lead into the jungle, which seemed to shudder and, as if with a massive effort, at once to absorb all, even this: from a hidden pillbox a machine gun began rattling gently beneath the din, and two men fell back into the ditch, one wounded, the other dead.

Weinstein was the first to reach the shack, with its two windows staring idiotically at the charging soldiers; he threw a grenade through each casement in explosive housecleaning. Then the others were beside him, the sun beating down upon their backs as they clustered in the building's lee gratefully.

In the open field the tanks stopped firing. The enemy lay silent beneath the verdant shield. The men panted against the comforting wall of the shack, waiting.

"Well, shit fire."

"Did they get that fucking machine gun?"

"You said it."

"Crocker. I want you to take your squad around the building and try and rush the edge of the woods. The Brownings will cover you. I don't know whether those sons of bitches are really stopped or not, but I don't much like the smell of this."

"Hey. Where the hell are those tanks going?"

"Right."

"Greenleaf?"

"Don't sweat it, Weinstein."

"Ayuh."

"What's it look like out there?"

"Thanks for pulling me out of the water that time."

"Looks peaceful as hell, Lieutenant."

"Shit, Wilson. Don't say nothing about that."

The tanks were pulling back in the face of the silence, believing perhaps that their work was complete, retreating through Barrigada now for a new assignment. At both corners of the shack's south wall the Brownings took position, Greenleaf's at the southwest; behind him crouched Crocker's squad preparing to make their break. The BAR gunners fired bursts into the jungle. There was no response.

"Looks clear, guys. Let's move," said Crocker. As they darted past him, Greenleaf saw from the corner of his eye the last tank disappear into the town.

And at that instant the forest came alive once more: snipers and machine gunners cracking and chattering, newly augmented by long thin whistles of mortar shells swinging down like small shiny chariots over the vicinity of the green shack, coming for to carry me home, O Lord.

The seven-man squad dropped to the dirt like stones, three of them hit. The BARs returned fire as the men who could began crawling back; then with a burst of unthinking fury Greenleaf bolted up and over his gun fifteen feet to where Crocker lay face down and still, dragged him by his belt to shelter behind the shack while Wilson and Weinstein pulled in the other two casualties. It wasn't until he was under cover that Greenleaf noticed his own left hand bleeding.

"Holy Christ."

"Let's see him, Greenleaf. Is he dead?"

"Spray the treetops. Try to knock off some of them fucking snipers."

"How's your hand there?"

"His helmet got clipped. Knocked him out, I think."

"Crocker. Wake up."

"Ain't nothing serious."

"No shit. Look at that dent."

"Ooooh."

"These guys are hurt pretty bad, Lieutenant."

"Those mortars are starting to find the range. We got to get out of here. Anyone want to volunteer to go and bring those tanks back?"

"Ooooh. What the hell happened?"

"Jesus."

"You're okay, Crocker."

"I'll go get them, Lieutenant."

"We'd sure appreciate it, Greenleaf."

He struggled out of his pack and squatted beside Wilson, who was giving first aid to the man he had pulled back. "Hey. Wilson."

"Yeah?"

"Take the Browning. You guys will need the firepower."

"Yeah, but—"

"I can't shoot the damn thing anyway."

At the lieutenant's signal, the men at the corners of the shack—as well as several who had taken positions inside—began firing into the jungle. Bending at the waist, the rag around his hand fluttering like a small banner, Greenleaf simultaneously broke: due west from the shack into the sun, across the twenty yards of scarred and pitted ground to the road, jerky and quick yet to him excruciatingly slow since his volition so far outsped his performance that he seemed to himself to be moving haltingly, lethargically. But finally with some grace he dived into the ditch.

He lay prone in soft mud, breathing deeply. Then he started to squirm south along the ditch toward the town. When bullets whined near his head, he realized he was partially exposed and flattened himself into the warm muck like a toad. He squinted ahead five yards to where the field swaled and the ditch emptied into it. No cover at all. But he saw that a twenty-inch culvert opened onto the swale from the other side of the road.

With rapid eel-like thrusts he worked his way to the mouth of the culvert and jackknifed himself into the black narrow opening, arms stretched ahead of him. With a momentary vision of being shot in the buttocks, he shuddered and wriggled quickly the rest of the way inside. "I guess two assholes would make one too many," he said aloud, his voice hollow in the narrow cavern. "Hah." Ahead he could see light, but faint and shapeless rather than a patch of round brightness. Something blocked the way.

He had almost reached the end of the culvert when with his right hand he touched something metallic—a helmet—and beyond that something else, at once plastic and unyielding: the body of a dead soldier. Bracing himself with his knees and feet, he pushed against it. Very slightly it started, gave way, moved, backed out at his pressure. Inch, push, inch, push, and at last the sluggish cork of what had once been Jack Walker fell out into the tropical afternoon.

"Aw shit, Jack." He crawled out of the culvert and knelt in the ditch beside the body, feeling for a heartbeat. When he gave up, his hand was greasy with blood. "Shit, now. Shit."

The face was devoid of all expression, wiped clean not only of agony and terror but of everything else too: pity, intelligence, cupidity, humor, hope, frailty, compassion; a face not so much at peace as at rest, in the manner of a fallen tree.

Still kneeling, he felt himself grow remote and isolated from the war. From a great distance he looked down upon the body, cold ashes, like an eagle sighting coldly down through rarefied upper air. Higher, higher: the dead man was ant sized now and shrinking. Greenleaf's eyes began slowly to close.

With a jerk he suddenly fell forward on his bandaged hand and with the other started slapping the corpse's face, across with his palm (which was as red with Walker's blood as his wrapped left was with his own) and then back with the back of it, again and again, tears falling from his eyes but with no sound, only the steady tattoo of the hand striking the face. Then that too ceased; and in silence he looked down at the empty, indifferent features.

When he got to his feet at last, he remembered his mission and resumed it. He had little trouble returning the rest of the way to headquarters, where he obtained the tanks and another platoon to assist in the removal of casualties. Withdrawal from the area of the green shack was completed by 1800 hours. The next morning, 3 August, it was discovered that during the night the Japanese forces had abandoned their positions northeast of Barrigada, and the town was secured.

4

SUNRISE strikes young my eyes awake, lights dustspecks above the bed above the floor hanging, drifting lazy bastids that we are. Flexing, yawnandstretch, brought short: bladder calls me out orders me out—battle without words rages. I lose. I give up. Up. Up.

"Goddamnit, Alcott. You wake yet?"

The oldman's voice rough as pinebark, old baster, The Old Ice-cutter (he never stops talking about it)—talk back to him but not nature. Must pee. Up and atem. What is today, a cold Wednesday. Two days past rabbit-rabbit. Shit yes, big day: birthday, November 3 of '43, seventeen and a man. Christ but all, even men, must pee. Out!

"About goddamned time."

At table he sits unshaved now in four days watching me. Fast feet, streaking past and out back, cold ground on bare soles, frosty breath in the air and now steaming gush across the firmfrozen earth, bright sparkling yellow. Sweet hollow relief, hallowed name. Prayer, hah. Old my father. Who fart at table. Inside.

"Eat your breakfast. We got a big day."

The oatmeal gleams like grease, cooling and now hardening. Hate it. No reason why we eat it, slippery lumps and goo, except oldman, his habit. Prison food. How to escape this trap, how to speak, how to raise my voice, which even now bows to his words:

"That so?"

"Ayuh. I got a line on a wrecked car down to Sheepscot. We're going down and haul it home."

He looks at me, dares me to call him a bluffer, to buck him, old baster. No birthday today my young son, does he say? or has he forgot the whole thing. His son the wife-killer, mother-murderer: did he love my mother? No, he rejoices in freedom, wants for nothing, hates none (at least not me), loves me? He has forgot.

"Go on. Get dressed. I'll start the truck."

Old gimper hurries out, the one boot smoothtopped, the other wrinkled, the loadcarrier. Why the rush, the car so important, must be a Cadillac at least or better. Birthday present? Not fucking likely. Dress slow, don't give in, silence is always better, is golden, sunshine, my pee. The strength of trees their silence. Where are my boots, here: put root in boot. This tree can walk but won't talk. Much.

Honk!

Coming! old fart, old baster, wrinkled cock. Ice-cutter: when you die, they'll burn ice in hell.

Old truck roaring, farting white exhaust in cold morning, great gassy engine. Good thing antifreeze. He sits at the wheel waiting, grinding gears (teeth too, probably). Climbing in through rust, dust, perching over the hole in floorboards over the road. No muffler, the motor howls, in cities a loud motor not allowed. Too loud. To be heard. Except the oldman. Who shouts:

"Ready, boy?"

Nod. And the truck jerks, roars, clashes, and we bounce out in bright cold morning, chains clanging on the blocks. The road unrolls past fields and stands of trees—birches, maples—who now have lost leaves and stand bare. But do not speak.

Fences, farms, houses, the church spire at Head Tide. Never went. Prayed only at goddamned school. Our Father. Who fart in Heaven. We pass in thunder but slowly toward Alna and the bridge, there cross the shimmering river, rocks shining below. On Wiscasset Road now a pickup, familiar green Chevrolet, approaches us.

Honk!

Honk!

Horace Barker, the oldman's bestfriend, waves to us and we also to him and each flash the other by. Horace a good man, the landgiver, but still we owe him, can't escape. What birthday present will someone give me. None. What you most want you must take. Nothing comes free.

Make left turn now to cross second bridge, to cross again the river. Pull up by Walbridge General Store gas pumps, like two roundheaded posts with their fingers in their ears. He cuts the engine. We get out and go in the store, deaf. Power of silence.

Inside, quiet also until a thin voice pipes at us:

"Goddamn. Eustis. How you been?"

"Middling, Wally. You?"

They talk, the old basters, two of a kind, easy words rising and falling like ducks on water, across which also drifts myself, but apart. The store warm and dim with its shelves of tools and cans and loaves of bread, cases of cigarettes and bubble gum and Necco Wafers and Nigger Babies. But wait; they call me.

"You know my boy? Alcott, this is Mr. Walbridge. Last year, Wally, he went and quit school and come into the business to help me out. I don't move quite so fast as I used to, you know."

Dried white face, false teeth. Smile and shake, don't speak. Done.

"Guess none of us do, at that."

"Ayuh. Well, we come down to pick up a car some clown ran off the river road yesterday. You know about it?"

"Ayup. Fellow named Jenson. Great big Pontiac. About a mile from here in a saltwater bog. Can't miss it."

"Good enough. Thanks, Wally."

"You bet. See you, Eustis. You too, son."

Blinking into chill breeze and shiny sun, we step and stumble. The gimper scrapes across the gravel, climbs in, turns key, tromps starter; we slam doors under cover of exploding motor. Timber on accelerator, wooden leg with a lead foot. We bounce along the road to where the river grows to bay, bright blue with whitecaps like chips and shards of broken glass.

The oldman pulls on wheel, brakes, stops, shuts off motor. Outside. The cold wind blows fresh across the water at us. No trees here. The car nosed down into the bog with shiny dark blue trunk in the air, like a fat lady stuck headfirst in a barrel. Anyone hurt, ask? Yes.

"Anyone hurt?"

"Naw. Lucky bastard was thrown out. He was drunk as a billybob, to boot. Now you back that truck around here to where we can get a chain onto it."

Lucky ducky bet your ass, that Jenson, lucky son of a bitch, son of a father, too. Like me. (Start, damnit. There.) Drunk and driving away fast, the coward should have stayed and fought. Why so? How does he hold me here, what chains me here, chains that don't change. Chains off the old block. Who now shouts:

"Good right there, bub. Chock them rear wheels."

See him pull chain thirty feet to Pontiac, old gimper, two wrecks down there now instead of one. Must follow old fellow, old father; together we strain with blocks and rusty chain, brown grass bowing beside us. Block wheels spin, chain rises, grows taut. Pull. We fling chain behind us, growing loop from the blocks that inch together, the Pontiac quivers, aching to come out, big blue tooth. Sucking sound from the mud. The oldman in front sweating, bending down, shirt out, pants below the crack of his ass. Straightens and turns to me, mouth open to speak:

TINGTHWACK!

Oldman crash at me blocks drop back fall sky—

"Umph! Hey. What?"

"Goddamned fucking chain. Broke."

Hurt?

"You hurt?"

"I don't know."

He stands, kicks. His right foot falls off. Boot lies in brown grass, pant leg flaps.

"Hah. Broke my timber in half. That's all. Give me a hand."

Give him my hand he says. Forever. Chains. Give a hand. Handy. Must speak:

"It's my birthday, today."

"That so?"

I will speak.

"I'm seventeen. I'm leaving. Going into the Army."

He don't look at me, hops once, picks up foot. Speaks to it:

"I could use you around here. You could use this car here."

No. His weakness is his strength; wooden leg the one he kicks with. I will not bend. Burn ice in hell, oldman.

"It's my birthday."

I walk away to Wiscasset. My strength still silence. Old ice-cutter, baster, gimper, man; old my father: let me go. How can I break free from you. Must I yet cut out my heart?

5

A week after the battle at Barrigada, on August 10, 1944, the pursuit phase of the attack on Guam was ended, leaving only various mop-up operations. Of the 18,500 Japanese troops estimated to have been on the island, 10,971 were officially listed as dead; the remainder had been either taken prisoner, killed in such a way that they could not be counted, or driven into the jungle to hide (one, a Lieutenant Hiroo Onoda, waited thirty years before finally surrendering on March 10, 1974). Of the 54,891 invading Americans, 1,283 were killed, 5,719 wounded, and 329 missing.

Greenleaf's company, for the past week deployed in corps reserve, was still headquartered in Barrigada when the campaign was declared at an end. At 1200 hours on that day Second Lieutenant Barton brought his men together, speaking to them with a stiff formality that did not quite conceal pride and pleasure and, quite possibly, relief.

"I want to congratulate you men on the way you have conducted yourselves during this entire operation. I want you to know that I've gotten compliments on the Second Platoon's performance. I'm very pleased.

"Also, on behalf of the whole platoon I want to thank publicly Corporal Alcott Greenleaf for his heroic actions on 2 August. I have recommended Corporal Greenleaf for a Silver Star; and whether Washington decides to award it or not, we all know that he deserves it."

The lieutenant smiled. "Oh. Yes. Perhaps Corporal Greenleaf will be able to wipe that stupid expression from his ugly face if he consults the General Orders, which have just been posted by my tent, where his promotion to corporal is clearly indicated.

"Dismissed."

The men surrounded him:

"All right, now."

"Let's hear it for the little corporal!"

"Christ, get him a drink."

"Speech!"

"Nice job, Greenleaf."

"Let me shake his hand. Give me your hand, boy."

"You're a hero, fellow. A real hero. The folks back home are going to be real proud of you."

"Give me your hand."

He endured their attentions stolidly without speaking or even smiling. When they at last broke into small groups and fell away chattering, he walked to his tent and sat down. He pulled a grenade from his pack and tossed it up and down in his right hand like a baseball. There was a small bandage on the back of his left.

"Hey, Corporal. Goddamned nice work." It was Wilson.

He did not look up. "Ayuh."

"No shit. You really deserve that star. I mean it. You should get it."

"That so?"

"Why, sure. Jesus, Mary, and Joseph. A Silver Star. Shit, I'd give anything to pin one of them on my mother when I get home. She'd be proud as hell. She'd love it."

"Ayuh?"

"Goddamned right."

"Jesus Christ."

Wilson flushed. "Well, wouldn't yours?"

"I don't know. You got a father?" Greenleaf stared intently into the dirt, as if Wilson might have scratched the answer there with a stick.

"No. He left home right after I was born. I'm all she's got."

"Ayuh."

"She brought me up right, though, by God. Made me go to Mass every week. School, catechism, too."

"She give you that ring you was talking about?"

"Hah? Oh, yeah. My father gave it to her."

"It's a goddamned piece of chain." Greenleaf suddenly unfastened his watch from his left wrist and stuffed it into his pack.

"What?"

"Jesus Christ, Wilson. I tell you. Cut it off and throw it away."

Startled, Wilson watched him stand up and walk toward the jungle. Only then did he notice that he carried no rifle, but in his right hand a grenade.

And afterward—after Greenleaf had disappeared into the dense undergrowth; after the subsequent explosion, faint and thin in the distance; after he came walking carefully and silently out of the jungle holding his left arm, handless now and bleeding, across his chest and the stump above his heart; and much later, after infection and fever caused him to be removed four thousand miles to a hospital at Pearl Harbor, and thus from all further contact with the Third Battalion—Wilson would say only that he was a good soldier, the best he ever knew, and must have had a reason for doing what he did.

VI Father and Son

ICARUS AND IPHIGENIA

Gaze with darkened eyes into the fire,
As rolling smoke drives toward an empty sky,
And taste in time the remnants of desire.

The sons who sunward soar, and ever higher,
(Their fathers watch—who taught whom to fly?)
Gaze with darkened eyes into the fire.

Thrusting, beating—their wings of wax and wire
Must finally burn. They fall, to bleed and dry
And taste in time the remnants of desire.

Other fathers, having lit the pyre,
Their virgin daughters too confused to cry,
Gaze with darkened eyes into the fire.

Fed by tides of blood, those flames soon tire,
And scores of blackened breasts will then reply,
And taste in time the remnants of desire.

In aching silence, child beside the sire,
Forever mute they stand, not knowing why,
Gaze with darkened eyes into the fire,
And taste in time the remnants of desire.

1

THE years spun out like weavings in an endless carpet unrolling, chasing Greenleaf and the others ahead and then covering their tracks behind them. Time marked each person in his flight—each save perhaps the son Eustis, revealed at last as an idiot, whose mind had been shut down at birth, a tangled cord crimping all understanding from his head at the same instant it crimped blood; who could at four years take a few shaky steps but who would never utter a sentence as long as he lived; who therefore was both freed from some changes and oblivious to all others; indeed, whose only hope of recognizing the passage of time would be if he should somehow happen to notice its cessation (as if at his death he might realize that the gears were grinding down and might say—or think, or know—I am not myself anymore). But even that possibility was not likely, and certainly neither Greenleaf, Margaret, nor Evelyn ever paused to consider it.

Initially, of course, they did not know about the child's damaged brain and so they simply absorbed him into the family circle, reacting to his presence in characteristic ways. Evelyn generally ignored him, refusing to acknowledge his existence except to complain of it once in a while; but Margaret threw herself joyfully into the task of catering to his squalling fussy infancy. Greenleaf said little, but set about reestablishing the family business in earnest.

After quitting his job in Wiscasset the day following the birth, his first concern was to restore the old Pontiac: take it down from the blocks, hammer out its fender, install in it new points and plugs, clean its carburetor, paint over its patriotic slogans, supply it with gas and oil and tires, and give it to Evelyn so that she could continue to travel to and from work. Margaret watched the transformation calmly, indifferently, and made no mention of her presumed ownership of the vehicle. The doomed tones of her pregnancy had disappeared entirely since the birth of her son.

The sun shone warm the day the Pontiac was finally ready. When Evelyn first climbed haughtily into the driver's seat, her body settled deep into the soft cushions and she found herself peering through the steering wheel. She turned to Greenleaf beside her. "I don't need any damn lessons, you know. I drove lots of cars before."

"Ayuh. Guess they all had higher seats, though." He reached into the back and brought forward a small pillow, which she slipped under her bottom. He sat back and watched as she put in the clutch, turned the key, and pushed the starter. The motor caught easily, she gunned it, and—wet mud and gravel spraying from under the wheels—they were off and flying, her eyes bright and intense, her accelerator foot straining to the floor, Greenleaf grinning with delight as they pounded up the road for North Whitefield and beyond, arriving—somehow—at Cooper's Mills. Across the bridge to his left he could see Ewen's General Store.

"Hey. Go across and by the store. Let's see if the pond road is open."

They turned right just after the store onto a muddy, potholed road, and again she stretched her foot to the floor. "Slow down, Evelyn. I broke a truck axle on this road once." They bumped hard. "See? You want this thing to keep running, don't you?" She slowed.

"Why do you want to come here?"

He did not answer. Outside, the floor of the woods was still mostly covered with spring snow—wet, sullied, granular—although in places patches of ground had broken through. Buds glistened on alders; evergreens shone in the sun. Through the bare branches of hardwoods, they could see Long Pond, white and blue and smooth. "Stop," he said.

"Why?"

"Stop."

She stopped by a field that sloped down to the pond, which gleamed in the sunshine like a huge mirror set in a brilliant frame. He opened the door and stepped onto the running board. "Come on." Without waiting, he jumped into the snow and began running toward the pond. In an instant she was after him. The snow broke beneath every step they took, and they wallowed knee-deep through it. With a *whumph!* Evelyn tripped forward face first into a drift of wet slush. From the shoreline Greenleaf looked back at her joyfully.

"Ho, sissy. That ain't how you're supposed to do it."

"Goddamn. What are we doing this for, anyways?" She picked herself up and came the rest of the way down, her white shirt plastered wetly against her breasts.

He pointed a short distance down the lake. "Look."

"What? I don't see nothing."

"See that mound of snow by them pine trees?"

"Yeah."

"That."

"Well, what is it?"

"Not 'is it,' sissy; 'was it.' 'What was it?' That used to be an ice house. I burned it down the night after my old man died. Burned some others too. I ain't been back here since that night."

She stared in silence at the mound he had indicated. The sun beat upon them warmly. His perceptions were acute; he could hear the snow settling and the water beneath it trickling into the pond, could smell the heavy wet air rising from the snow's sparkling surface. From a nearby pine a red squirrel chattered angrily at them, at something. Then she spun to face him.

"Goddamnit all. Just goddamnit." With an angry shake of her head, she sent quick tears flying from her eyes like water from a dog's back.

Suddenly she was sobbing and clinging to him, nearly clawing him, her damp breasts pressing into his chest, as he patted her back in astonishment. It was five minutes before she began to calm, but eventually he got her up the hill and into the car and at last home. He did not understand what had caused this outburst, but he knew enough not to tell Margaret about it; and in a week or so it was forgotten, displaced by Margaret's hoarse crooning in his newborn son's ear and Evelyn's satisfied driving in his dead father's automobile.

So the three of them passed one year and then another, each secretly watching the child more and more narrowly, waiting for some sign that he was developing in a way other than physical size. He swelled and lengthened and at last stood up, but his face never lost its quality of soft, pale amorphousness, its mushroomlike color and texture—a face quite capable of framing certain expressions (fear, pain, anger, repose), but, with the dreadful honesty of an idiot mind, totally unable to lie about any of them. Still, however, they said nothing of it. By the time he was four, they seemed to be in a circle dancing intricately together over him, being always careful not to tread upon him; yet like accomplished Mexican hatdancers they appeared not even to look at the focus of their movement.

Even while they were not admitting the existence of the child's increasingly apparent amentia, its presence was spawning in the Greenleafs an unconscious antisociality. Although two or three nights a week Evelyn would return from dates smelling of beer and tobacco and perfume (in her own car—her men picked her up at work and she drove herself home), he and Margaret no longer saw anyone, not even the Grotes or the Wares. Their only outside intercourse was commercial—his buying and selling the used parts, or her occasional shopping. Usually, though, Margaret stayed at home keeping company with Eustis, her radio, and (after 1952) the television set—miraculous instrument!—suddenly animate, bristling with life after its two dusty years of dormancy. She and the baby watched it virtually from test pattern to test pattern. Greenleaf would come stamping in at suppertime to find them sitting on the couch like bookends, engrossed with Clarabelle squirting seltzer water all over Buffalo Bob, or Howdy arguing patiently with Phineas T. Bluster. Both viewers assumed an identical expression of a thoughtful fish with open mouth and wide eyes; neither ever laughed or smiled or reacted in any other way to what transpired on the tiny flickering screen. He would stand behind the couch, watching it with them until Evelyn came home from work (or until six o'clock on the nights she had dates), and then would go into the kitchen to serve whatever meal Margaret had found time to gather together during station breaks and advertisements.

During and after supper the four of them would sit there mute, bathing in the news and the channel's other nighttime offerings. It didn't matter what it was. They received Portland's Channel 6 better than the others, so usually they spent the evening entertained by the National Broadcasting Company. They would have been just as happy with the Columbia, or—had it been available to them—the American.

To Eustis the television could not have been more than a cabineted lamp flickering bluely against his face and making noises at him. Yet from the moment it was turned on he sat docilely in front of it, soaking in the light like divine grace, an infantile and moronic Buddha contemplating this electronic luminosity as if it were an extra-personal navel, apt subject of his sober omphaloskepsis. (In fact, he was drawn to all moving brilliances, to all shimmerings: accidental prisms and rainbows; flashes of sunshine from water or traveling cars; Tinker-Belle reflections from morning cups of coffee, flitting and trembling against walls; and most of all fires—candles, gas jets, cigarette lighters, and burning logs. In the presence of any of these he sat enthralled, not moving toward it or any other way either, unblinking and fascinated, a sluggish, mindless moth without wings.)

Thursday, the first of April, 1954, was the opening day of fishing season in most of Maine. Elsewhere, President Dwight D. Eisenhower was signing into existence the United States Air Force Academy; scientist J. Robert Oppenheimer, the developer of the atomic bomb, was about to be stripped of his government security clearance; Atomic Energy Commission Chairman Lewis Strauss was proudly showing off his new hydrogen bomb; Chief Justice Earl Warren was preparing to listen to the arguments for both the Topeka Board of Education and a small black child named Brown; and Senator Joseph McCarthy was getting ready to wage his final war, this one against Communist sympathizers he perceived to constitute much of the higher echelons of the United States Army. Great waves these, yet they lapped but gently upon Greenleaf's shores. When he walked into the house after work this day, Margaret was in the kitchen, Eustis was sitting on the couch looking at a lighted candle, and the television set was turned off.

"Margaret?"

"What?"

"What's the boy doing in here?"

"Oh, nothing. The candle keeps him quiet, that's all."

"I see it does. But suppose he knocks it over?" He stepped into the kitchen. "What's that?"

The air was warm, perfumed with baked chocolate and sugar. Margaret stood at the counter holding a bowl in one hand and a tableknife in the other. With the knife she was swirling frothy waves of white frosting over a huge black boulder of a cake. Beside it lay four thick stubby hurricane candles. She smiled at him with unusual gaiety, flour and confectioner's sugar dusting her face and arms like talcum powder.

"It's his birthday."

"Ayuh. So it is. We going to have a party?"

"Well—you and me and Evelyn and him. That's all."

Just then the Pontiac pulled into the yard outside. "Here she is," he said. "Early." He looked through the window and added, "Uh-oh."

Evelyn's face was screwed tight with anger. When she stepped around the car, he could see her lips pressed flat against her teeth. Halfway to the house she stopped, picked up a stone, and whirling about—flung it back at the automobile. He saw the passenger window grow suddenly a star, and a faint crash reached his ears. "Well. Goddamn. I guess today might not be all that cheery for the boy, after all."

She banged into the living room. "Goddamnit, what's this?" From the kitchen they could hear a sudden puff and then an immediate howl from the child. "Oh, shut up. You'd like to burn us all to ashes, wouldn't you?" Still howling, barely a click. "Hang on, will you? What's wrong with this goddamned television?" Then a fluttering noise, the howling's instant cessation, and "—Howdy Doody time, It's Howdy Doody time . . ."

He looked at Margaret. "What we got for supper?"

"Boiled dinner."

"Ayuh. Well, we might as well get to it."

Without further conversation they filled and carried three plates into the living room. Evelyn did not acknowledge their presence—nor that of the boiled dinner, for that matter—but only sat glowering at the screen as if she wanted to throw a rock at it just as she had at the car window. Margaret sat beside Eustis, feeding herself and occasionally poking a forkful of boiled potato or carrot or pot roast into his mouth. He did not take his eyes from the screen to notice where the food was coming from but just sat there, opening and closing his mouth like an aspirating trout, his supper apparently passing into it without his knowledge or suggestion. For his part, Greenleaf sat on a chair separate from the others with his plate balanced delicately on his knees. Generally his eyes were downcast, though once in a while they strayed to the television screen, where lately Buffalo Bob's face had been replaced alternately by those of Senator McCarthy and a newscaster.

When they had all finished save Evelyn, who continued to ignore her food, Margaret rose and carried the empty plates into the kitchen. From there she called, "Alcott. You want to shut off the television?"

He stood and clicked the screen blank. The child blinked in surprise, then opened his mouth. Before he could begin crying, however, Greenleaf saw small flames flashing from the kitchen door and said, "Hold it. There. Look at that, Eustis."

The howling died unborn in his throat as Margaret swept in with the cake, flames from the four candles shining and dancing toward them out of the darkness. Eustis sat gaping and still, bathed in the fire's glory, appearing perhaps as the face of Lot's wife might have looked at the instant of her metamorphosis. Then Evelyn spoke.

"How come he gets a birthday cake?"

"Why, it's his birthday," answered Margaret.

"So what? It don't matter to him about that."

The child continued to stare at the candles, oblivious, timeless.

"What do you mean?"

"He don't know it! Goddamnit, you're just as bad as he is, Margaret. Honest to God. He don't know one day from the next. He's four years old and he can't talk—can't hardly walk—can't do nothing except make drool and turn good food into shit. He's a dummy. Goddamnit. He ain't got the brains of Howdy Doody. And you won't even admit it. Either one of you. Jesus! Sometimes I think you're both as crazy as he is."

As she stood up abruptly, her sister spoke. "Look, Evelyn. Just because you had a hard day at work, you don't have to bring your troubles home to us."

"Look, yourself!" she shouted. She bent like an angel or a stooping kite over the cake and blew. With a flap the flames were ripped from the candle ends, leaving four wicks that glowed and smoldered in the dark. An instant of horrified silence and then the thin agonized shriek of the child.

"Look at that!" screamed Evelyn over the din. "That's your son! Goddamnit all, anyway!"

She stood furiously over them. Slowly, patiently, Greenleaf pulled his Zippo from his pocket, thumbed it open, and spun the flintwheel. Small fire jumped from the flame guard. He stretched out to relight the candles, and as he did so Eustis subsided. There was an instant of silence after he snapped the lighter shut; then he placed it—shining silver!—in the child's unresisting hands. "Happy birthday, son."

Evelyn began laughing. "What'd you give him that for? He can't use it. He can't even drink his own milk by himself. Ha. Ha." She went over to switch on the television set, then sat back on the couch.

Eustis was staring at the cigarette lighter in his hands. He did not appear to notice when Greenleaf squeezed out the candles with his thumb and forefinger or when the bright images flickered across the screen before him. His fascination with his present was so intense and somehow purposeful that his father and mother both perceived it and sat watching silently. He turned the Zippo in his hands once. Then he pulled back the cover. At this sight Greenleaf felt his heart bound with astonishment and joy; and as the case clicked faintly on its spring, Evelyn whirled from the television as if at a rifle shot. All three of them sat stock still, gaping in amazement at the child, from whose mouth even now hung suspended a thread of drool that glistened in the bluish light. He had the open lighter in his left hand, holding it upright before him with the cover flipped back over his thumb toward his wrist; with the extended first finger of his right hand he reached out and touched the flintwheel, delicately, deliberately, like a tiny unmitered bishop at a baptism; and as the trio of adults sat around him riveted and wordless, he spun the wheel down and away with his finger—all the while staring at his gift out of vacant, half-closed eyes. It was as if he had no idea at all of what his hands were doing. Nonetheless there was a spark, a slight cough, and sudden fire that burned brilliantly above his hand like a torch.

"Goddamn," said Evelyn. She turned off the television, and they sat there for perhaps five minutes, the four of them gazing into the small flame.

Finally it began to sputter and shortly afterward, with a *pop!* that seemed too loud, went out altogether. Even then Eustis did not let go of it, but simply opened his mouth wide and began to cry. Greenleaf said, "Here, boy. Let me have that. I'll put some more juice in it." He took the lighter from the small hand— "Jesus. This thing is hot"—and went into the kitchen.

"Shush up. Eustis. Here, I'm turning on the television." In a minute Groucho Marx's cartoonish face appeared on the screen: "—magic woid and the little boid'll come down and pay yer a hundred dollars—" and Eustis subsided. When his father returned with the lighter, he was quiet, absorbed in the bluish dots in front of him, and did not even seem to notice the silver rectangle as it was put into his lap.

And that was that. They never again saw him use the lighter, though he carried it with him everywhere he went. Margaret made him a lanyard, to which Greenleaf was able to attach it; and the child wore this around his neck almost all the time, even when he slept. In the first few weeks that followed, the adults watched him closely for some further indication of ripening intelligence but could discern nothing. Eventually they came to a tacit conclusion that Evelyn had been right, that the child was indeed feeble-minded and that they had simply been privy to a small but cosmically inspired April Fool: and they did not speak of the boy's fourth birthday again.

2

WHEN Greenleaf looked out the door the next morning, the first thing he saw was the Pontiac, its star-splintered window staring reproachfully back at him. He turned inside, noticed Evelyn's door still closed, and moved toward it. He rapped. "Evelyn." When there was no answer, he pulled it open.

The room was dim and redolent with faint musk. She lay on her side, nude, apparently asleep. Most of the covers had been thrown back; part of one leg was under the sheet but the rest of her body was stretched out gracefully like a statue upon the bed. He stood in the doorway, frozen in a mixture of surprise and terror and lust, staring with sudden intensity at her sleeping and naked vulnerability: the breasts, the buttocks, the dark patches of hair at the pubis and the armpits.

His heart began to pound and his breath caught in his throat. At last, after what seemed a long time, his arm passed slowly across his body, and he saw the door shut in front of him without even realizing he had moved it. Closing his eyes, he inhaled deeply; then he rapped again at the door and called, this time more loudly: "Evelyn! Get up! You're late for work!"

The voice that came through the door was awake and full of ire, with no trace of grogginess. "I ain't going to work."

"What?"

"I ain't going."

"That so? How come? You sick?"

"I quit it."

"That so?"

From within the room came a series of bumping noises, and then the door swung open. Evelyn, wearing a ratty bathrobe, glared out. "I just quit it. I was sick of it, that's all." She slammed the door.

So now they were all together during the days (and the nights, too, for she had also, it seemed, given up her social life along with her employment: the telephone would ring for her once in a while, but she would speak into it with curt low monosyllables, and after a while the men ceased their calls). At first it was hard for Greenleaf to admit to any changes around the place other than the obvious one of a second female presence constantly there. The daily routines mostly continued as before. The same day Evelyn first stayed home, he drove to Wiscasset and returned with a thick sheet of glass and several boxes of wire, bulbs, and other hardware. Having first replaced the window, he spent the afternoon under the hood and floor of the Pontiac, screwing and wiring fixtures, and then over the top of it, washing and rubbing Simonize to a shining luster. Then he went back to the house, where the two women and the child sat like furniture in front of the television.

"Hey, sissy."

Evelyn looked up quickly, suspiciously.

"Come outside."

She rose; together they went into the yard where the Pontiac stood gleaming like a dark jewel in the late sun.

"You fixed the window."

"That ain't all. Look." He led her to the rear and, going to the driver's side, reached in. The left brake light began to blink and synchronously with it a second red light newly mounted inside the rear window.

She looked at him seriously, like a child evaluating a parent, and asked, "How come you put them on?"

"Direction signals. You use them instead of sticking your hand out the window."

"I ain't going to use them."

"That so?" He felt an unexpected pang of disappointment, but kept his voice and face noncommittal as he turned away. An instant later she spoke again, her voice soft yet intense.

"They are okay, though. They look pretty good."

A wave of pleasure ran through him. Then he walked back to the house, to his wife, to supper.

Margaret soon began feeling the oppression of her sister's personality continuously haunting the house. When out of sorts, Evelyn could obscure a room like dense fog; and when the women were together she seemed seldom to be happy. Mornings, with Greenleaf gone off working, she would from time to time indulge herself in low, venomous monologues aimed apparently at the television set, stacatto, disjointed, yet delivered in such a way that Margaret could not help but hear: "I give anything to get out of this goddamned dump. Her and that dumb kid, I swear to Christ. Ought to go up to the city, that's the ticket. This hole stinks. Old cow don't keep the shit off the floor. No way. Now that's a living room, by God. Makes this one look like puke." Meanwhile Margaret would duck by her, desperately dusting or sweeping or mopping, always trying to stay out of the way of her malevolence and never quite succeeding. Later in the afternoons, all three—the two sisters and Eustis—would be in front of the screen, each lost in response to the image illuminating it. Greenleaf would find them this way, clustered about the set like flies at a jammy table, when he came in at the end of the day.

The first difference he became conscious of after Evelyn's demission from the Busy Bee was merely that his household seemed cleaner, better managed than it had been since Eustis's birth. His work clothes started coming to him starched and pressed, his suppers prompt and hot; and he was pleased. More often than not it was Evelyn who served him—she would leap from the couch when he entered, rushing to the kitchen to rattle some dishes and slap Margaret's dinner onto plates and carry his meal to him with untoward grace and graciousness, switching her hips from side to side, wearing an expression of intense concentration—and so for a while he allowed himself to believe that she was responsible for many, even most, of these changes, that she was with her own hands performing nearly all of these services.

Toward the end of that April, in defense, Margaret began a campaign of spring housecleaning. Bringing out buckets and rags and a stepladder and brushes and Ajax, placing Evelyn and Eustis and everything else in the center of the rooms, she set to washing the walls of the living room and the kitchen. She did the kitchen first, scrubbing away grime as if it were sin or disease, then restored order there before moving into the room where, among an aggregation of chairs and tables, her sister and son sat watching tiny glowing shapes dance before them.

She started by the kitchen door and washed steadily around the back wall past the bedroom doors until she came to the chimney. With a small brush she began at the top to scour the bricks, each separately, with great patience and care, like a brooding hen turning her eggs. Slowly she worked down the chimney until she was just above the skeletal leg of her late father-in-law.

"Hey!"

She spun at the sharp word, almost losing her balance. Evelyn was glaring at her.

"What are you doing?"

Margaret looked at her, helplessly, hopelessly.

"You ain't supposed to frig with that leg. He said so. You told me."

With a jerk Margaret snapped closed her mouth. Then she turned back to the bricks, her shoulders trembling. But she did not try further to clean near the leg.

When Greenleaf entered the house, he found Evelyn and Eustis at the television. From behind the closed door of his and Margaret's bedroom he could hear a series of dull whaps, each punctuated with a muffled grunt.

"What's that, sissy?" When she made no sign of having heard him, he kicked her foot. "Hey. Sissy. What's that noise?"

Whap! Whap!

"What?" Evelyn smiled at him, and he felt suddenly weak kneed and foolish.

Whap!

"What's that?"

"Oh, Christ. *That.* Margaret, the old cow. That ugly old

cow." And with that same dazzling smile she looked back at the television screen to be enveloped in its flickering aura, instantly shutting him from her presence.

He turned, eyes narrowing. The soft explosions continued, regular as a metronome. He walked to the door and stood stiffly in front of it.

Whap!

Evelyn spoke from behind him. "Go on. Open it. See what she's doing. The old cow."

Gently, noiselessly he turned the knob and pushed open the door. Margaret's back was before him, her cotton dress damp with sweat down the spine. As he watched, she raised a broken broomstick over her head like a double-bitted axe and with a grunt slammed it down onto the bed *whap!* and again *whap!* and then he closed the door, slowly turned back to the television set and to Evelyn, who was watching him intently.

"Alcott."

At last he answered. "Ayuh."

"I ain't your sissy. Don't call me that no more." She smiled upon him a third time, and once more he felt weak as a baby.

And so, although he did not articulate the realization to himself, Greenleaf began to see that the ecology of his household was shifting. Margaret said nothing about it to him, said nothing to anyone, spending all her days in desperate housework, all her nights in the mindless wash of television and sleep. Evelyn spoke more often to him and smiled as she did so, but her words concerned mostly what she saw on the television, never what she or her sister did during the day. He himself said as little as possible to either, skating between the frozen surfaces the two women presented each other. He began going to bed early. When he awoke each morning,

Margaret would be lying asleep beside him, snoring softly, her fists clenched and eyes screwed tight like those of a raging infant.

Late one afternoon, he entered the house and found that Margaret was not in the living room, and he could tell by the lack of kitchen smells that no dinner had been cooked. Evelyn jumped up. "Margaret's sick. She went to bed. We can go out tonight to eat our dinner."

"She sick, you say?"

"We can go in my car."

He looked in upon his wife. She lay on her side in the bed, covers pulled up to her ear, facing the wall, unmoving. After a minute or so he closed the door. Evelyn had already gathered up Eustis, who was protesting limply at the loss of the television light, and they were almost out the door. "Wait up," he called, but she continued on, so he ran out after her.

In the yard sat the Pontiac. By the time he reached it she was already inside, jabbing at the starter, Eustis sitting quietly on the seat beside her. He opened the passenger door just as she hit the accelerator and, hopping onto the running board, managed to pull himself aboard. Stones spewed from under the tires, spraying the façade of the house.

It was not yet eight o'clock when they returned home, twilight settling over them, spring peepers chirping at their ears. Inside, he put fresh diapers on the seat of his son, set him in the crib from which he could watch the television set if he wished (assuming he possessed enough volition to decide; if he did not, weakness or electrical failure or other circumstance would determine whether he watched or slept), and with no further word to Evelyn—who was already seated beyond recall in front of the set—went into the gloom of his bedroom, where his wife lay still as death in their bed. Undressing, he climbed in beside her. She was awake. He could hear the tension like electricity singing away within her and finally spoke to it.

"We were at the Busy Bee. It was pretty fair. You okay?"

"Alcott. I think I'm going to go visit Lin and Bessie for a couple of days." Her voice, low, hollow with desperation, was barely audible.

"Hah?"

"It'll be a rest. I can take Eustis and go for the weekend."

All at once he felt his head swimming. He answered carefully, "Why, sure, Margaret. Say, why don't you leave the boy here? Evelyn and I can handle him okay. You can have your vacation from all of us."

"I just wish she'd get right out of this house."

"Evelyn? Goddamn, Margaret. She's your sister. You can kick her out if you want."

"I want to ask Lin and Bessie about it."

"Ayuh. But I'll say this. She sure seems to be helping some around here. The house has been looking real good since she quit work."

"Well, if it has," said Margaret bitterly, "she's been doing all her helping with that hateful mouth of hers."

He was amazed. Her frank admission of hostility toward her sister was strange enough, but now the eventuality of his spending a weekend virtually alone with her bowled him over. He could not rid himself of the memory of her nude on her bed and so lay awake beside his wife in awe at the emotions whirling and churning within him: excitement and concupiscence and exhilaration and fear and guilt.

This was Wednesday night. Until Friday he seethed inwardly but was able to mask it with frenetic work, which had an additional advantage of leaving him so exhausted on the intervening night that he had no strength to toss and turn in bed. On Thursday he brought home and stripped to its bent and broken chassis a ruined Ford, leaving the motor on the shop floor and every other salvageable part arranged on the bench, all as clean as God and man could make them; the next day he brought in a second Ford, this the victim of a cracked engine block and three years of wintery neglect, and was well on his way toward a synthesis of the two when Margaret wandered out to the shop to find him.

"Alcott. I got my bag packed."

"Ayuh."

He crawled from under the chassis and went into the house to wash his hand and face. When he came out, he was carrying her bag. She noticed that he had brushed his hair back neatly.

"We can take Evelyn's car."

They rode in the Pontiac through the bright April afternoon, he oppressed and stifled in his wife's presence, she rigid and morose in his. An interminable forty-five minutes later they rolled across the Kennebec River and turned off Route 1 onto Front Street. When Margaret stepped out beneath the faded green sign—"Mary's Diner: The Best Cup of Coffee in Bath"—she waved sadly back at him; he nodded smiling at her and sped away, leaving her on the sidewalk holding her cardboard suitcase and staring after him. All the way back to North Whitefield he hummed and whistled.

He did not enter the house when he got back, but instead parked the car and went deliberately into the shop. There he worked until five thirty, at which time he walked briskly up to the house, entered through the kitchen door, and washed himself for the second time that afternoon. As he came at last into the living room, clean and flushed, his heart was pounding so loudly in his ears that he could scarcely hear the sound of the television.

On the end of the couch nearer to the set sat Eustis, completely absorbed as always with the cold blue light in the cabinet. On the other end, apparently as intent as her nephew, lay Evelyn—smoking a filter-tipped cigarette, legs extended langorously over a small table in front of her, now expelling a stream of smoke from pursed and red-glossed lips, wearing black lace lingerie, bra and panties and nothing else, save only the silver necklace he had given her several Christmases before. She took no notice of him, but continued to look at the lighted screen through her hooded eyes.

He stood over her, hardly able to speak, breathing heavily until he was able to rasp, "What you doing?"

Although she did not look up at him, after a pause she stood and crushed out the cigarette. "Come on." Still avoiding his eyes, she crossed slowly to his and Margaret's bedroom door, undulating her hips as she moved in almost a caricature of sexual heat. She turned and saw that he had not budged. "Come *on,*" she repeated impatiently.

With a mental swipe he knocked away all the lumber jumbled up in his mind—faces (his wife's, his son's, his dead father's), objects (the television set, the Pontiac, the skeletal leg hanging over the mantel)—and followed her in, leaving the son unblinking and oblivious on the couch. He traveled helplessly, mindlessly, without volition or decision, swept along as if on a river of fire. Somehow he stumbled out of his clothes, reached the bed, and then fell upon her.

Afterward he could remember only vaguely what happened next: their frenzied couplings no sooner finished than recommenced, her fingernails raking his back, her pantings and gruntings, his tumescent penis scored by the electric hair of her pubis. There was no sense of gratification or of release—only of caustic urgency. They did not speak even a word to each other until at last he fell away from her, spent and exhausted, like a used artillery shell or a dead cicada.

Then she said, "Good."

The word resonated around him in the dark air. He felt all its nuances—self-satisfaction, pride, arrogance, cupidity, recalcitrance—but he was too empty to respond to any of them. He just lay on his back staring up at the black ceiling. There was a click as she snapped on the bedside lamp and light filled the room.

"You like being a junkman?"

"It's okay."

"It don't sound like much. Junk."

"Well, auto selvege, then."

"Auto selvege?" She thought it over. "You was in the war, wasn't you? A hero."

"I wasn't no hero."

"You get a check from them."

"Ayuh."

"Well, how'd you lose your hand?"

He did not answer.

"Didn't you do something brave?"

After a pause he replied, "I guess not much."

"Margaret thinks so, don't she?"

He nodded.

"Good." Again the tone of self-satisfaction and triumph. Then she reached down to stroke once more his shriveled penis. At her touch it jerked, became erect, flamed red; and she said, "Come on. Do it again."

He pushed himself up onto his side and ran his stump down over her breasts and navel to her crotch. Desire pulsed through him like a shock, dispelling all fatigue. He rolled atop and with sudden strength pushed into her. In the midst of his rut, however, for some reason he happened to look toward the open door where, staring wide-eyed at his copulating father and aunt, stood Eustis. His expression was void as space; but to Greenleaf it seemed full of horrified comprehension, like that of a doom-speaking prophet at an Armageddon—who can only gaze mutely toward tumbling towers in the moment of his vindication.

3

ALONG the April road in majesty came a new Cadillac. Royal Azure was the manufacturer's name for its color, and sunlight glinted from its waxed enamel and chrome surfaces like bright bolts of fire. Although its wide whitewall tires bumped generously in and out of potholes, the automobile itself proceeded smoothly, a great flagship under way through small seas.

Inside Margaret was saying, "Gee, Lin. It sure rides good."

"Don't it? I think it's a corker. I like it a lot better than my old one."

She leaned back against the cushions. "It was nice to visit. The restaurant looks real good. And I feel a lot better about talking with you."

From the middle of the seat between her and Lindall, Bessie said in her prim, shrill, skinny voice, "Heavens. Any time. We're more than glad to see you. And don't forget what I told you." Reaching out, she clicked a knob in front of her, and they rode most of the remaining trip in aural comfort, too, entertained by the spring warbling of the new car's new radio. "Come on-a my house," sang Rosemary Clooney. And thus they continued until, coming around the final curve to the Greenleaf house, they were confronted with a sparkling new sign, white with gold and black lettering, set precisely in the same spot its careworn predecessor had occupied for nearly twenty years: GREENLEAF AUTO SEL-

VEGE. USED PARTS—REBUILT MOTERS. ALCOTT GREENLEAF, PROP.

"Look at that, will you?"

"Ain't that classy."

"Wonder when he found time to make that?"

As the Cadillac pulled into the yard like a huge wheeled sapphire, Greenleaf stepped out from his shed to meet it. He put his hand over his eyes, elaborately pantomiming blindness, and gaped his mouth in mock astonishment.

"God, Lindall, that's a real blister you got there. Why, hell's bells. Let's have a look at it. Christ almighty! Automatic transmission, power brakes, power steering. Power windows, I bet, too. Probably got everything on it except a television, and there's a plug in the back seat for that. Hah? How big's the engine?"

Lindall had never heard him talk so much at one time. "Huh? Oh, hell, Alcott, I don't know nothing about motors."

Bessie spoke up. "Say, that sure is a nifty sign out there."

He flushed and smiled simultaneously. "Ain't it. Shows up good." Then as an afterthought, "Evelyn made it."

There was a shocked silence. At last Margaret broke it: "How's Eustis? He give you any trouble?"

"Not a bit. He's inside watching the television with Evelyn. Say, Lindall, Bessie. Come in for coffee? Beer?"

"Well, thanks, but we really got to get back to Bath. And we got to stop off by Westport on the way."

"That so? Huh. Lots of Greenleafs over to Westport. No relation to me, though. I don't think. You sure you can't stay?" All the time he faced them, his mouth was set in a thin smile, unwavering and metallic. He did not speak quickly, but there was a soft urgency in his short sentences, a quiet despair.

He stood watching as they each in turn kissed Margaret on the cheek, climbed into the Cadillac, and drove away in clouds of dust and glory. Then he followed her into the house.

Inside, Evelyn and Eustis sat on the couch in the shrouded living room, the television reflecting over their faces like moonlight. Neither was dressed: the child in his pajama tops and diapers, the woman in her scruffy bathrobe. Margaret raised the shades and light streamed in. When she stepped in front of the couch, Greenleaf saw her lips were pressed close together; then she snapped off the set. Eustis began to howl.

"Hush!" she shouted, and miraculously he hushed, not in any way astonished or frightened, but simply stopped, as if his mother had pulled a plug from an electric socket and left him like the television set, without power. Then she turned to her sister, her voice rasping with anger. "Evelyn, look at you. It's five in the afternoon and you ain't even dressed yet. Eustis ain't either. You just been sitting around here like always in front of the damn television the whole damn day, getting white as a codfish and fat as a sow in summer. There ain't no need of it. None at all."

Evelyn's expressions shifted kaleidoscopically from white astonishment to flushed anger to pink disgust while she listened to this harangue, but before she could reply, Greenleaf cut in ahead of her: "Hell, Margaret. She done a lot this weekend. She painted that sign for me."

She looked at him with her brown eyes almost frozen in their sockets. "I see that."

And she was out of the room and into the kitchen, banging pots and pans together like cymbals, leaving the two of them looking at each other with wary wonder, until finally he spoke in a quiet voice. "Goddamn. Margaret don't talk like that."

"She ain't going to talk to me that way."

"I wonder what the Grotes said to her?"

"She thinks she is hot shit—"

"Evelyn—"

"—but she is only cold piss."

"—that ain't no way to talk."

"Alcott."

"Hush." He rose and switched on the television set. There was a humming, then electronic snow, and finally resolution into a mahogany hearing room: men seated at oak tables, papers and microphones arranged before them, the camera already closing on one among this company, dark and round and swarthy and malevolent, who stood up gesticulating and shouting, "Point of order! Point of order!" Greenleaf was moving to change the picture when she said, "Wait."

He stopped. "What do you care about him?"

"I want to look at him." He sat again as she continued, "He is going to get rid of them damn Communists. There's too many Communists in the Army, and he is going to put them all in jail."

"He don't know what a Communist is. There ain't any Communists in the Army."

"How do you know? You wasn't a war hero. You said it. You don't know nothing about the Army. He was a fighting Marine. They call him Wisconsin's Fighting Marine. He knows all about the goddamned Army."

He glared at her as he stood to change the channel. The screen clicked through rectangles of snow until a fuzzy picture of a man on a motorcycle appeared, and a voice said, "—because, Mrs. Thompson, you asked for it!" Then the motorcycle began roaring down a ramp.

Nonchalantly she rummaged through the pockets of her bathrobe and removed a package of cigarettes. Drawing one from it with her lips, she leaned over to her nephew, who did not look away from the roaring motorcycle as she took hold of the lighter dangling from his neck. She lit the cigarette, her head bent close to the child, then straightened up to face Greenleaf. Her eyes were wide, shining with sudden excitement. "Alcott. Was you a Communist?"

"Hah?"

"You was, wasn't you. In the Army. I bet you was a Communist."

He stared over at her, saw her leaning forward expectantly, the cigarette held close to her half-opened lips. "Hell, Evelyn. I wasn't nothing like that."

"Supper is ready." From the door Margaret's words splashed over them like yesterday's dishwater. "Tonight we are going to eat it in the kitchen."

"Why?" demanded Evelyn. "I want to watch the television."

Greenleaf pushed himself up from his chair in confusion. "Wait. Margaret, what's got into you? I never heard you talk like this before."

The words poured out of her like corrosives from a cracking vat, bitter and angry. "I'll tell you what. It's her! Ever since she got fired from that job at the Busy Bee—that's right, fired! Lin heard the whole story, told me all about it. She got caught stealing money from the cash register. More than a hundred dollars, Lin says. And now she don't do a damn thing but sit around here with hardly no clothes on like some Portland whore. I had enough. From now on she's going to straighten out around here, or I'll know why." Abruptly she ceased speaking and looked furiously at both of them, not so much subsiding as clamping herself shut. Neither of them had ever before seen her so angry.

There was a pause, palpable, and then Evelyn rose gracefully, languidly, before them all—sister and nephew and brother-in-law/lover—and sliding the bathrobe off her shoulders, let it fall to the floor. She stood for what seemed a long time before them without moving, naked and demure. (Only Eustis ignored her and steadily watched the television set, where Jack Barker was again saying, "You asked for it.") Finally she spoke, her measured words wrenching them asunder and instantly reducing Margaret to tears, Greenleaf to tatters, as the words hung brightly in the air like brimstone over Sodom: innocently she asked, "Alcott. You old Communist. When are you going to throw this bitch out?"

4

So the next day he took Evelyn, Eustis, and some blankets and moved into the old Pontiac.

Evelyn's simple question had smashed to bits not merely his marriage but the entire order of his life; and he seemed now to leap recklessly into squalor, borne down perhaps by the combined weight of the woman and the child, leaping not with reasoned deliberation but neither without cause, much like a boar sent into rapacious transports at breaking down and entering a corn-filled sty. The first morning he drove to town in his truck, returning with many cases of beer and a few of canned food, most of which he set in the trunk of his new home. Then he and Evelyn began successive rounds of drinking, eating, copulating, and sleeping in the back of the automobile, with the son sitting either in the front or on the ground outside as stolid and insentient as a sack of grain.

None of them reentered the house while Margaret was in it, and left alone, she did not stay there long. For the first two days of her grass widowhood she did not even appear at the window, much less step outside, and no lights showed at night. Then on the third morning they saw her open the door and emerge carrying her cardboard suitcase and a large shopping bag. Although she was dressed in her best suit and coat, she had the appearance of being somehow bulkier, more massive than usual. Without looking at the automobile—to say nothing of its occupants—she went straight to the road and with that strange obese dignity began walking toward Wiscasset. All at once he realized that she seemed fat because she was wearing not one dress but many, that the two bags contained everything else she could both lay claim to and carry, and that she was not planning to return.

As soon as she was out of sight around the bend, Evelyn said, "Good. She's gone. Let's move back inside."

When at first he did not reply, she opened the door and climbed out. "No," he said.

"What?"

"No. If you don't care for it, you can leave, but we ain't moving back inside that house."

"But I want to watch the television." When he said nothing more, she grew shriller. "Goddamnit. It ain't fair. She ain't coming back. She don't want the house. How come you won't let us move in it?" He opened a can of beer and sucked deeply from it.

A sunburst of understanding broke across her face. "Because you're still scared of her. That's it, ain't it? You think she's still in the house—or some part of her is, anyhow. And now you ain't man enough to face up to her or even the part of her that might be left, or to what you done to either one of them."

He set the beer on the floorboards, stepped out, and stood facing her. Her nostrils flared angrily at him. Then his hand whipped out like a snake and slapped twice—*whapwhap!*—

across her cheeks and mouth. Her head snapped back and tears sprang into her eyes.

"Bastid!" And she was at him, her extended and rigid nails clawing out at his face, her feet kicking, her head bobbing and butting. He was forced back against the automobile. One of her hands raked across his face; with his own he fended her off and then swung his handless arm like a club over her head, and she sprawled on the ground sobbing and panting.

That was all of it. They continued to live in the Pontiac, the three of them while the spring grew more certainly toward summer. Two or three times a week Greenleaf would leave in the truck, usually returning with beer and maybe food (once in a while a peck of clams, which they would steam over a fire in front of the car. Once someone, some occasional junk customer who happened by and found them at one of these feasts, came away with a description of the scene: "She was setting there with her legs flopping out of that car wearing her underwear and some goddamned bathrobe that hadn't been washed or mended since it was made maybe a dozen years ago, drinking beer and gobbling up them clams. The kid set on the ground in a dirty diaper, with a cigarette lighter hanging from around his neck and his mouth gawked open like a baby robin's; and every now and then Greenleaf would lean over and drop a clam into that open mouth—like a pebble down a well, don't you know—and the kid would swallow and open up his craw again. I never see nothing like it.").

He made no pretense of continuing actively to work. Initially he was able to keep them in beer and food with his monthly disability check. But this resource was insufficient to maintain them for long in their new style of living, and halfway through the month of May he woke up to the astounding fact that there was nothing left in his wallet, that all his money had vanished, most of it for the beer that they were now consuming at the rate of well over a case a day. A second revelation, however, immediately followed the first: during all the years of his marriage to her sister, Evelyn had been secretly squirreling away a store.

"You got to get some more beer," she said one afternoon.

"I ain't got the money. We're broke." He grinned at her.

"Nothing?"

He shook his head, still grinning.

"Wait." With deliberate steps she went up to and entered the house. When she came out she was carrying something in her hand. "Here. Get some other kind. I don't like that Schlitz much. And some cigarettes." She handed him a crisp twenty-dollar bill.

"Where'd you get this?"

"I got some money. I got it hid where no one can find it. Hurry up now." She gave him a quick triumphant smile and added, "When you get back, I'll be in the house watching the television."

So he had been bought, and he knew it. There was no actual gesture of obeisance, no oath of indenture; but he clearly saw that the mere twenty dollars had put him in permanent and irrevocable bondage to this woman, and no longer could he prevent her from doing anything to which she set her mind. When he returned in an hour or so with the beer, Eustis was sitting alone in the slanting sunlight of late afternoon, watching tree shadows dance on the ground around him. There was no sign of Evelyn, except that the door to the house stood ajar. He sat down beside the boy and opened a can of Budweiser.

Even after this resounding victory for Evelyn, they did not move back into the house. True, during the days she would now recline inside on the couch drinking beer and watching television, but when "Howdy Doody" came on at five thirty she would shut it off and tromp down to the Pontiac for food, more beer, and nocturnal copulation. Greenleaf—who continued to refuse to enter the house—thus found his days once more his own. Even his drinking abated somewhat, and he often carried his son through the woods to the river to fish. Eustis would sit on a rock in what might have been some ecstatic and transcendent state of illumination, watching the water shining brightly as it riffled over small stones in the shallows, or the scales glinting as a fish wriggled in his father's hand. Gradually, then, Greenleaf's new life took shape—a succession of static images rather than the earlier organic process of growth with Margaret: images of his mistress sprawled beerily in front of the television, of himself poised with rod over the river, of the two of them coupling in the back seat of the Pontiac, or of his son seated wherever he was set, inert yet always responsive to light, gazing with empty eyes on sunshine like some bit of phototropic vegetation.

In such estate were they when in late afternoon of the summer solstice Sheriff Bartholomew Ware drove into the yard at the wheel of a brand-new Nash that was starred and initialed and shining with glory. Greenleaf was on the running board of the Pontiac cleaning some trout, holding them belly up between his knees, slitting them, with his thumb flipping the viscera into the driveway, and dropping the hollow bodies into a pail of water. Eustis was near him. Piles of clamshells were scattered all about the driveway, and they forced the sheriff to pick his way carefully as he stepped toward them.

Greenleaf smiled wanly. "Hey, Sheriff." He dipped his

hand into the pail and wiped it on his pants as he stood up.

"How are you, Alcott? Happened to be up this way, and thought I'd stop by." He shook the damp hand without demur.

"Business?"

"Naw. Just wanted to see how you fellows was getting along."

"See you got a new car, too."

"Ayuh. The old one finally gave up."

"Ayuh." He stood there, arms folded over his chest, smiling at the sheriff.

"Ain't seen much of you lately. Guess it was what, last Christmas? We was really glad you come down to see us then." He pulled out a handkerchief and wiped his forehead. "Say, Alcott. Me and Emmy was awful sorry to hear about your troubles. If there's anything we can do, you know—" He turned his palms up in a gesture of futility.

Greenleaf kept smiling. "I guess we're doing okay, Sheriff. Thanks, though."

From the house the door banged. The men watched as Evelyn in her bathrobe came out and with unsteady deliberateness walked toward them. No one spoke until she had almost reached the Pontiac.

"Howdy, Evelyn."

"Well, hello, Sheriff. You come out here to arrest Alcott?"

"Nope. Why? What's he done?"

"He's a Communist."

The sheriff laughed shortly. "Oh. I guess that ain't my territory."

"He is. I'm going to write to the Wisconsin Fighting Marine about him." Her face was serious, intense.

"Now, I'll tell you. That man wouldn't know a Communist from a cuckoo clock. He is just bad news. Or he was. After Friday I'd say his time is up. That lawyer Welsh just tore him apart. Thank the Lord."

She grew red, then whirled and stamped away behind the Pontiac. Suddenly she squatted out of their line of vision, and they heard a splattering of angry urination over the ground. The sheriff flushed and looked away—at the idiot son, the offal-covered driveway. When he spoke, his voice was soft and old and tired, as if it was coming from a great distance or across a great span of years. "You know, I never did get to know your father very good. They say he could be a strange fellow, not easy at all. But in his way he was goddamned proud of this place. I know he was even prouder of you."

Greenleaf continued to stare at him, the smile unwavering.

"There was a time," said the sheriff, "when I guess he had reason to be." He turned abruptly and strode through the clamshells to his new car. Behind him in the hot afternoon sun the smile had frozen to Greenleaf's face like a mask of ice.

5

LOVE, to each his own, a rose must remain with the sun, old father stumps next door. Not yet in bed? Angry, upset, worse. Old baster. He don't know the half.

My life. Mine. My hand. My heart. Gave him one hand, save the other for Margaret. What about my heart? Only one. Sheets wind me up, this bed's my grave. Suck. Suck! My hard heart. Weasels suck eggs. Pop. Goes. To each his own. What good is a song. Love?

—You didn't, he says. —No son of mine, he says. Damn!

Soft, those tits. Who wants the whole? the hole. Fuck for

luck. Cherry, mine. Have never. Wanted. No, liar that I am, I want the whole/hole thing, but clean sheets, not in this dirt. Must I marry for it, for them?

In the clean-sheeted hospitals I never said what happened. No one knew for sure. Got disability, almost a purpleheart, another to break. I won't talk again. Never. The words just don't belong. Let them think what they want.

I will have a son who will not speak at all. I speak only to break my father's pride. Bastid. Broke his heart. (There in the next room I hear him stumpstirring.)

I will show him.

He will love Margaret. She could not stop singing that song. Must be past midnight, now August 31, 1946, tomorrow rabbitrabbit. I need the luck.

—You're a war hero, he says. —You're my son. You watch out for them damn women. But he don't know her, the old baster. Don't know the half.

I will tell him. The son must remain with the rose. Not with the father.

Why did I tell him? He knows.

When Margaret lies beside me in the fields I feel her titburied heart beat. No fear. She won't let me. My cock rises, spits in my pants, falls. This must be love, must be, must.

Wrinkled cock. But what did I say to him? (We got along great when I didn't tell him nothing. Then he was proud of me, loved me.)

What did I say? (Do I hear him moan?)

What?

I said—I ain't no fucking warhero. I said—nobody shot my hand off, goddamnit. I blew it off myself with a grenade. That's all I said. Oh, goddamnit. How white his face. He never knew. And I could never tell him why I did it.

To each his own.

Tomorrow I will tell him that I leave him my father to go take Margaret my wife. We will have a buster of a fight. Fires. Tomorrow. Will burn like bombs.

6

AFTER the sheriff departed, he and the woman quarreled bitterly and conclusively. She left him as empty as the discarded skin of a snake, standing by the automobile. "You ain't too good to spend my money, you bastid," she had screamed at him. "I got better than three thousand hid up in that shack you call a house, and that's good enough for you and that goddamned sheriff, too, you bet."

"I can guess how you got all that money."

"What's it to you how I got it? You ain't too proud to take it. I'm moving back inside the house. For good."

"No, you ain't."

"You just stop me, mister." Pausing briefly to snatch two six-packs from the open truck, she stalked up to the front door, stamped inside, and slammed it shut behind her.

He sat down on the ground, helpless and—for the first time in his life—utterly incapable of response. All emotional heat, all anger and lust and pride and ferocity and scorn, had escaped shimmering into the frozen black regions of sky where stars glitter like tiny chips of ice. Beside the Pontiac in the dirt he slumped in a sort of catatonia, the night of this longest day gently and silently falling over him, the house, the car; over trees, land, river, and sea. It was as if he had, like some prismatic Fourth-of-July sparkler, burned to the end of his wire and had here at last in the dying twilight gone out.

After a time there came a sound, a high wail, thin and mindless. At first he took no notice, but it increased in volume until he was forced to rouse himself. "Why, sure," he said hopelessly and, getting to his feet, went to the rear of the Pontiac. It was too dark to see inside the trunk, so he brought the crying child to his side and snapped open the Zippo. It lit easily and Eustis hushed while by its light Greenleaf picked out a can of baked beans. This he held between his knees and punctured with a beer-can opener. The two sat side by side, father and son, taking alternate bites from the can. After they finished, he lay back against the car, looking up at the dark house. The empty can slipped from his fingers and without even realizing it he fell asleep.

His consciousness dropped like a stone so far and fast that his sleep was untroubled by either the mares or any other dream-bearers. He did not hear Eustis beside him begin to cry, so when the child, still crying, stumbled away toward the house, it was hardly to be expected that the resultant quiet should disturb him. Night sounds enveloped him softly: frogs and peepers, insects, from somewhere a lunatic whippoorwill, all singing their distant songs into his oblivious ears; then along the road came an anonymous and unmuffled automobile thundering past him, the Pontiac, and the house. Still he slept on, out of reach of all sound.

But not of all light. When at last he opened his eyes, he was doubly confused because he had not realized he had fallen asleep and, having done so, he did not now understand why he was awake. Seconds passed before he sufficiently collected his wits to think to himself, Something's wrong, while light flickered across his face. The house! Flames were already piercing the roof and belching bright sparks upward. He lay there for an instant longer astounded, agape: this structure, which had stood for all of his twenty-seven years and more, which had housed both his father and his son and all the women in his life besides, which had been privy to most of the quarrels and couplings and births and deaths of his life, was here and now exploding into the night sky. Then he smelled the smoke, olfactory confirmation for his boggling vision; and he was up and running toward it.

It seemed to him that he was still asleep but now dreaming, specifically that he was racing toward this conflagration in slow motion (just as he had when he had run from the Japanese fire on Guam), as if held back by some invisible yet potent hand that pressed against his chest and slowed him to an awkward lumber. Sheets of flame curtained the living room windows, lively and quick fabrics. The smoke grew richer and ranker as he finally closed on the door (actually, he had been less than five seconds in crossing the thirty-some yards from the Pontiac) and with a last gasp of outside air he threw it open and jumped into the room.

Behind him came a rush of air—*whoosh!*—and above the roof the flames leaped higher. Much of the smoke that had filled the room was swept up and out as well, and in an instant of clarity he saw the entire scene in tableau: Evelyn on the couch apparently asleep; the television set sitting in a nest of fire, still radiating a bluish test pattern like a block of ice in a burning bush; flames dancing, eating at the floor and furniture, running up the walls and out the roof; and directly in front of him, in the midst of a circle wonderfully untouched by the fire, Eustis—the open but now flameless Zippo in his hand, his mouth likewise open in an expression of serene amazement, beatific awe.

"Evelyn!" he shouted, and just then—*bang!*—the television's picture tube exploded. She began to stir and cough, for by now the smoke was again growing denser, the heat more intense. He scooped up the boy and turned for the door, calling once more, "Evelyn! Get out!" and coughing. Through gaps in the smoke he saw her standing up but with her back to him, scrabbling at the wall above the stove and mantel, digging for something behind the plaque that bore his father's leg; and then smoke rose all around him and his eyes burned and teared and he stumbled out gagging. As he set the boy on the ground, he could hear Evelyn shriek once inside; then all noise was subsumed in the snapping and crackling of the spruce timbers and pine boards while the Greenleafs, father and son, stood/sat by watching this, the final annealment, the last blessed fire of purification and release.

Acknowledgments

I confess myself particularly indebted to the following people, who contributed much expertise and information of which I would have been otherwise unaware: John C. Caldwell, Dr. Robert S. Carson, James A. MacCormick, and Gregory S. Payeur. Much thanks, too, to Louis O. Coxe for his invaluable suggestions and encouragement.